19.95

Ice Trek

ICE TREK

Ewan Clarkson

CENTURY
LONDON MELBOURNE AUCKLAND JOHANNESBURG

ACKNOWLEDGEMENTS

The extract from *The Ballad of East and West*
by Rudyard Kipling is used by kind permission
of the National Trust for Places of Historic Interest
or Natural Beauty and Methuen London Ltd

Copyright © Ewan Clarkson 1986

All rights reserved

First published in Great Britain in 1986 by
Century Hutchinson Ltd,
Brookmount House, 62–65 Chandos Place,
London WC2N 4NW

Century Hutchinson Publishing Group (Australia) Pty Ltd
16–22 Church Street, Hawthorn, Melbourne, Victoria 3122

Century Hutchinson Group (NZ) Ltd
32–34 View Road, PO Box 40–086, Glenfield, Auckland 10

Century Hutchinson Group (SA) Pty Ltd
PO Box 337, Bergvlei 2012, South Africa

British Library Cataloguing in Publication Data

Clarkson, Ewan
  Ice trek.
  I. Title
  823'.914[F]   PR6053.L36

ISBN 0-7126-1273-4

Typeset and printed in Great Britain by
WBC Print Ltd, Bristol

For there is neither East nor West,
Border, nor Breed, nor Birth,
When two strong men stand face to face,
tho' they come from the ends of the earth!

> *The Ballad of East and West*
> Rudyard Kipling

FOR REBECCA

1

An empty can, caught by the wind, rattled across the icy stones. The brief summer had passed. The sea was restless, stained with the blood of the dying sun, and the wind from the west was cold with the breath of the ice floes. They were not visible as yet. They lay beyond the horizon some thirty miles out to sea, but soon, Larsen knew, they would be prowling just off shore, jostling and growling amongst themselves like hungry beasts as they groped for a blind stranglehold on the land. There was no season of autumn as such in the Arctic, just a short blaze of colour as the leaves died. Then, in a matter of days, winter would reclaim the land.

East lay the wilderness, brooding and dark, a vast empty expanse of rolling hills and flat, desolate marsh, of bog myrtle, moss and cotton grass, and a few wind-bitten, sun-starved willows, an endless, roadless waste that was the tundra. Seemingly lifeless, inanimate, it appeared none the less to radiate a threat, an alien presence with the power to destroy.

Between, on a strip of land that lay curved like a bear's paw out into the sea, lay the settlement, a few prefabricated houses apparently dropped at random on the thin turf that flanked the shore. All around lay a chaotic litter of snow machines, dog sleds, dinghies and outboard motors. Some were in need of repair, others beyond it. Oil drums were everywhere, painted bright red for easy location from the air or in the snow, the ubiquitous 'Alaska Rose' that now blossomed from the shores of the Bering Strait to the Canadian border. Here and there drying frames for fish or hides, built of wind-fretted, sea-washed driftwood, stood skeletal against the sky. Empty now, they served as perches for the ravens that scavenged along the shingle shore, where shreds of torn plastic snapped and crackled in the wind.

The Eskimo settlement was almost deserted. Most of the men were away on summer employment, and the women had taken themselves, with their children and old folk, to summer camps, where they spent their time berry picking. Larsen pulled his parka hood over his cropped blond hair and, stepping gingerly between the dried dog droppings and mounds of decaying blubber that littered the shore above the tide line, picked his way to the shelter of an abandoned boat.

The boat stank, a ripe, rotten aroma of fish, whale oil, rotting meat and dog, but it was no worse than the rest of the shore. The people maintained their skill as marksmen by taking pot shots at passing gulls and mouldering corpses littered the tide line, their wings outstretched for the last time.

Larsen looked for somewhere to sit, decided against it, and squatted down on his haunches. It was a trick he had acquired in his time as a marine, during interminable days and nights spent surviving in damp, steaming jungles on the other side of the world. Even now, five years later, he could still squat for hours without discomfort.

For a long moment he gazed northward, his pale blue eyes watering a little with the effort, to where a series of flat ridges, ancient raised beaches, climbed steadily skywards towards hills that were shrouded in mist.

Earlier he had walked some way over those ridges, where for years archaeologists had scratched and burrowed in the permafrost, trying to piece together the lifestyle of generations of people who for thousands of years had made their homes there. He had picked up a flint arrow-head and rather guiltily shoved it in his pocket, knowing it was against the law. Yet it was not his violation of the Antiquities Act, which forbade the collection of native artefacts, that disturbed him. Rather, it was the knowledge that the arrow-head meant nothing to him, told him nothing about the man who had made it, who had fished and hunted and lived and loved, and eventually died there. Nothing, except that he was clever with his hands, and imbued with an instinct to survive.

For what? he pondered, looking out to sea. Once there had been a land bridge out there, linking Alaska with Siberia. Over the flat marshy plain hunters had journeyed, following the great game herds that were their livelihood. For ten, perhaps twenty thousand years men had endured the cold and hardship of this Arctic environment. The sea had risen, separating the two continents, but even these turbulent icy waters had proved no barrier. For centuries the people had crossed and recrossed the strait in frail skin boats, for trade, brides and barter. Now the continents and their peoples were divided by a power far greater than the forces of nature, an idea in the minds of men.

Larsen was accustomed to thinking of communism as a product of the East, while capitalism was of the West. Now he found himself in the topsy-turvy position of looking west towards communism, while capitalism lay behind him to the East. He was on the shores of a land whose people were the descendants of a culture older, longer lasting, better tried and tested than either of the other two. Now they were being tempted, coerced, into a monetarist system that might or might not sustain them. Meantime they were losing the skills which had enabled them to survive since long before the dawn of agriculture.

He felt in his pocket for the arrow-head and pulled it out into the light. It was tiny, exquisitely formed, like a leaf from a tree, the point still sharp enough to pierce the skin. Were all this endeavour, this ingenuity and invention to perish and be lost for ever, like the bones of the arrow-maker himself? Were the Eskimo culture and the hunting, fishing, foraging way of life to vanish, to be replaced only by the squalor he now saw surrounding him?

If so, it was a pity, the more so since he, Larsen, had hoped to cash in on that lifestyle before it disappeared entirely. He preferred to forget much of his war, especially the long, fear-filled, fever-ridden days he had spent in the jungles he had grown to hate. Yet there had been good times too, and a chance to travel, to visit exotic places he had not until then known existed. That he should enjoy the experience had come as a startling revelation to him, he who had grown up in the American Midwest, who had never even seen the sea, and who, as far as he could recollect, had never cherished any ambition to travel.

After his discharge the hunger for new places lingered like a tropical rash, an itch that would not heal. He reasoned that if he felt this way so too must numbers of others, and that they might be prepared to pay for the privilege. So he had set up his own travel agency, specializing in tours to out-of-the-way places, and he had proved himself right. The business was a success, and he could have expanded, but he preferred to stay small, to offer a personal service, and to charge highly for it. So he ran the agency on his own, or almost, for he had started with one girl assistant who was now a woman, and whom he now loved so much that he was strongly tempted to marry her.

Earlier that year he had learned that Congress was to create a number of new national parks and nature reserves in some of the remotest regions of Alaska. Of more interest to him was the news that the native peoples, the Eskimos and Indians, were to be allowed to retain their traditional rights to hunt and fish, and to continue, so far as they wished, to enjoy their subsistence lifestyle. It occurred to him that some wealthy white Americans might savour the combination of a wilderness experience and a chance to view the Eskimo way of life. So, as soon as he could spare the time, he had come north to explore the possibilities of such a tour. He had quickly been disillusioned.

The region was too remote, too inaccessible, the terrain too hazardous and the climate too harsh to tempt any but the very young, strong and adventurous. They could not afford the cost. There was also a distinct lack of the sort of amenities his clients had come to expect. He had discovered very early on that even the most elderly tourists would endure extreme privation during the day, as long as they were assured of a hot shower and a soft bed at the end of it. Here he could make no such promises.

Then there was the attitude of the people themselves, shy, reserved, unwilling to welcome intrusion. 'It's like this,' one of them had explained. 'I can't kill a seal to order, especially with a bunch of pointy-toed tourists breathing down my neck, and if I failed, I'd feel foolish. Again, suppose we were skinning and butchering a seal. Would you like it if you were fixing your car or working on your boat in your driveway, and a crowd of us gathered round to watch, laughing and taking photographs?' In spite of himself, Larsen had to admit the man had a point.

He had other doubts, too, and these he expressed out loud in a message to his assistant, speaking softly into the personal tape-recorder he always carried.

'Sylvie, honey, this is just about the end of the trip, and our hopes. There are no walrus, no polar bears, no caribou and no wolves, at least not within fifty miles, and these Eskimos, they don't look the part somehow, not a fur-lined parka among the lot of them. Most of them seem to be dressed in an assortment of government surplus clothing. Worse, those who are still hanging around here just aren't interested in tourists, or in trading souvenirs.'

He paused, wondering if he were painting too gloomy a picture, and decided he was not. One thing above all his clients expected was a range of native handicrafts they could bargain for and take to show the folks back home. He had had visions of carved walrus tusks and caribou antlers, sealskin mitts and boots, but nothing like this was on offer. There was one last chance. Away to the east, straddled asprawl the Arctic Circle, lay a mighty chain of mountains, the Brooks Range, effectively isolating the Arctic from southern Alaska. Deep in the heart of this mountain barrier, situated in a broad valley which bisected the range, and forming one of the few routes by which a man might pass from north to south, lay the tiny native settlement of Anaktuvuk.

There was no access by road or rail. The supply road to the oil fields at Prudhoe Bay lay even further to the east. The only way in to Anaktuvuk Pass was by air. Yet here, less than forty years ago, a group of Eskimos had settled down to live. Once they had been nomads, people of the deer, following the great herds of caribou on their spring and autumn migrations, dressing in their hides, living in tents of skin, feeding on the flesh and fat of the deer. Earlier in the century they had been driven north, betrayed by the scarcity of the deer on which their livelihood depended, to seek a living by the shores of the Beaufort Sea, to hunt the seal, the walrus and the whale.

Then the deer had returned to the hills, and so the

people had come home too, to hunt the caribou and the wild sheep and the bear. They also, so Larsen had been told, ran a profitable sideline in native souvenirs, which they sold in cities further south. The pilot of the plane he had chartered was willing to fly him there, and if, as Larsen feared, the place turned out to be as big a disappointment as this coastal settlement, then at least he would be halfway to Fairbanks and a jet service back to the States. He pressed the record button again.

'This has got to be the waste disposal unit of the western world, where all man's efforts get ground up and washed away by the sea. I'm flying back to civilization shortly and tomorrow I'm heading east about three hundred miles, to a place in the mountains where I'm told the natives carve souvenir masks. I'll bring one back for you. We might be able to arrange a package tour out there. In fact I expect I'll be back in the office myself before you get this tape, but I'll mail it for you anyway. Take care! Steve.'

He switched off the recorder and rose to his feet in one smooth movement, a long lanky Swede like his father and grandfather before him, a man fast approaching middle age but refusing as yet to admit it. For the first few steps he walked with a slight limp, a stiffness from a leg wound which had seemed trivial at first but which, in the foetid warmth of Vietnam, had refused to heal. Finally they had operated on his calf, cut away the ulcerated tissue and left him with barely a scar or a limp. Within a month he was walking twenty miles a day and now he had grown so used to the initial stiffness he was scarcely aware of it.

With his right shoulder hunched against the wind he began to walk briskly back along the dusty dirt trail that led toward the settlement. Already he could hear the first drone of the aircraft coming to collect him, and he felt thankful he would not have to linger long. A raven started up from a pile of rubbish by the track and honked derisively as it swept away on stiff black outstretched wings across the tundra. A solitary old man appeared at the door of one of the shacks, stared blankly at him for a long moment and then disappeared inside again, closing the door behind him.

Larsen shrugged and walked on. Even if the natives had been more friendly there were other insoluble problems. The peak of the tourist trade did not fit in with the seasonal pattern of hunting activity. The spring whaling and sealing were over, the autumn caribou hunt had yet to begin, and in July, he had been told, the bugs were unbearable. Berry picking moreover could hardly be classed as a tourist attraction, however important it might be to the natives.

The four-seater Cessna was waiting, poised like a small silver dragonfly on the airstrip. It was old, and bore a battered and bruised look. Some of the dents, though, were uniform, so that it looked as though the plane had flown through a barrage of golf balls. 'Hailstones,' the pilot had explained cheerfully. 'We run into them all the time.' Larsen shuddered. The knowledge that the pilot would have to apply at regular intervals for a certificate of airworthiness did nothing to calm his mind.

Tibbett, the pilot, was a Texan, though Larsen would not have guessed it. The man was so small he might have been a professional jockey. Handy, though, for a bush pilot, thought Larsen. The less pilot the plane has to carry, the heavier the freight it can bear. He was nearer to the truth than he realized.

The Texan was sitting at the controls of the plane when he arrived, chewing on the burnt-out stub of a cigar and reading a worn paperback. He threw away the cigar as Larsen climbed aboard, but the rank smell lingered. 'Find the North Pole then?' he queried.

'Didn't know it was lost,' grunted Larsen. 'Now if you could fly me to a scotch.'

'Like an Apache arrow, boy,' said Tibbett. 'Mind, it

will cost you. I swear that stuff's so precious by the time it's been freighted in that it's worth more than all the gold that came out of the Klondyke!'

Larsen let him ramble on. He had a bottle of scotch in his hotel room. He buckled on his seat belt as the engine roared reassuringly to life, and sat back in the cramped confines of the cabin, trying to relax and barely bothering to look down as the plane lurched and bounced a thousand feet above the tundra. He was tired and hungry, and the chill wind from the sea seemed to linger in his bones, making him feel old and somehow vulnerable.

The seaport was as squalid as the settlement, but busier, noisier and more crowded. He was grateful for the warm blast of air that hit him as he entered the hotel, which was run down and seedy, smelling of fish and fried bacon, unwashed humanity and warm wet wool, but at least his bed was comfortable and the food was good.

A new modern hotel was under construction close by, built out of some of the money awarded to the natives in partial settlement of their land claims. The half million square miles of wilderness, of forest and mountain, of river and swamp and lake and tundra, the sprawling frozen land mass that was called Alaska, the great land, was being carved up piecemeal. The state was acquiring about a third. The natives had settled for rather less than half that amount, but in addition they had received almost a billion dollars in compensation, money that was being managed now by regional corporations run by the natives themselves. Perhaps one day they would have a tourist industry after all.

Meantime, up in his room, Larsen took the bottle from his holdall, poured a generous measure into his toothmug, and lay back on the bed, feeling the warmth of the scotch flow through him. He was not as a rule a solitary drinker, but it was cheaper than drinking in the bar.

Since practically every essential of life up here had to be flown in, the cost of living was nearly twice what it was in the rest of America, that union of states referred to almost contemptuously by Alaskans as 'the lower forty-eight'. Such prices would have to be reflected in any sort of package deal. Another reason, he supposed, for considering the venture a non-starter. He poured himself another drink. After all, he wouldn't be needing the scotch much longer.

Dinner was good. Larsen chose reindeer steak, mainly because it was half the price of beef, and found it little different to the deer he had shot in the woods back home. After indulging an appetite keened by the Arctic air, and reluctant either to step outside or suffer the solitude of his room he made for the bar. He ordered a beer, wincing at the price, and leaning back surveyed the scene.

The air was thick with the haze of tobacco smoke and redolent with the fumes of alcohol. The clients were mostly Eskimo, fishermen betrayed by the reek of their clothing, construction workers in hard hats and thick tartan shirts. Others, Larsen guessed, were drinking their way through their social security cheques. A group of whites, probably oil men, played cards at a nearby table.

'Mr Larsen?'

The voice at his side made him start. The man, Larsen judged, was older than he, in spite of his lack of beard and cropped black hair. He had the high cheek-bones and dark slit eyes of an Eskimo, but he was tall, touching six feet, and thin almost to the point of emaciation. There was something else though, something odd, and it took a moment for Larsen to identify it. The man's nose was wrong for his face. It looked rather as though it belonged to an Indian. Larsen shrugged mentally. For all he knew, the man could be Japanese, or even Cantonese.

'My name is Umiak. It means whaleboat.' He giggled

nervously, as if he were accustomed to people laughing at the joke.

Larsen waited. What did you say to a man called whaleboat?

'You will forgive me.' It was an order rather than a request. 'I heard you were flying to Anaktuvuk in the morning, and your pilot has agreed to take me along.' He giggled again, irritatingly. 'I don't weigh much, and of course I will pay my share of the charter.'

Larsen shrugged. He felt irrationally annoyed that Tibbett should have done the deal behind his back, even though he would benefit financially. 'Welcome aboard, Mr Umiak,' was all he said.

He held out his hand. The man's grip was brief but firm and strong, the palm calloused and horny, the hand of a manual worker. Yet Umiak himself had the air of a leader, of an assurance flawed only by that nervous laugh. It came again, grating like a torn fingernail.

'What takes you to Anaktuvuk, Mr Larsen?'

For a moment Larsen was tempted to tell the stranger it was none of his business but then it occurred to him that the man could be a useful contact with the natives. So he explained.

Umiak was silent for a moment. 'Anaktuvuk is hardly a tourist resort, Mr Larsen. I personally hope it never becomes one. You might find some examples of native art, if the owners are willing to sell, but most of the inhabitants are too busy leading their own lives to perform for wealthy sightseers.'

Too busy sitting around getting smashed legless like this lot, thought Larsen. I'll get no help from this arrogant bastard. Before he could make any retort Umiak changed the subject. 'Our pilot seems to be enjoying himself.'

Larsen had not noticed the little Texan until then. He sat at a table in the corner, his shirt sleeves rolled up above the elbows, challenging all comers to an arm-wrestling contest. For a small man he seemed remarkably strong. He also seemed to be leaning rather heavily on the scotch, and Larsen said so.

Behind them the bartender gave a short rasping bark of a laugh. 'Don't worry about him, gentlemen. Drunk or sober, he couldn't pilot his way out of a paper bag.'

'He's survived longer than we thought,' observed Umiak reflectively. 'Maybe he's learning.'

They're trying to faze me, thought Larsen, and they're succeeding. 'He seems an experienced pilot,' he remarked mildly.

The bartender sniffed. 'He has a few hundred hours' flying time. Mostly crop spraying, in Alabama so I'm told.'

'Don't pay no attention, Mr Larsen,' said Umiak. 'I'm flying with him. What our friend means is this. All the very best pilots are taken on by the oil companies and big business concerns, because they pay top wages. The state and federal agencies have their own pilots and we have to make do with what is left. Some are good, some are bad. Our Texan friend is a lot better than some we've seen come and go.'

'He still has to get through a winter up here,' grunted the bartender. 'If he survives until the spring, he might make a bush pilot.'

'Anyway, I hear the forecast is good for tomorrow,' said Larsen.

Umiak shrugged. 'The stars were dancing when I came in. That means wind. Besides, the mountains breed their own weather. Still, all forms of transport are hazardous in this country. It's something you learn to live with. I'm told that the highways in the lower forty-eight can be quite dangerous.'

So, thought Larsen, can be a flight in a helicopter gunship over the jungle. He could not remember how many times he had sat, cramped and uncomfortable, his webbing chafing his skin and his carbine slippery in his grasp, wondering how many more such missions he could survive. Well, he'd come unscathed through them all, unless you counted the leg.

Umiak had drifted away to talk to someone further down the bar. Taking advantage of this a young Eskimo girl sidled over and whispered in his ear. He refused her offer more abruptly than he had meant to, and was startled to see her blush as she turned away discomfited. Imagine that, he thought to himself, an innocent hooker! She was pretty, though. How could he explain to her that she reminded him too much of other lovely young girls in the bars of Saigon, girls whose company he had enjoyed to the full, and whose fate he had never since allowed his mind to dwell on.

He looked into his empty glass. Another few beers and the girl's offer might sound too good to refuse. Maybe he ought to take advantage of it, before the oil men got bored with their cards. Instead he went up to his room, but he had finished the scotch before he was able to sleep.

2

Morning dawned bright and clear, but with a biting cold that numbed Larsen's fingers and struck an irrational chill of fear in him, for it seemed as if the icy claws of winter were reaching out to try to hold him prisoner in their grasp. Over breakfast he learned from the proprietor that Tibbett was already up and gone, and had left a message to join him at the plane. Of Umiak there was no sign, so Larsen set off alone, hoping the fresh air would clear the lingering whisky fumes from his head.

The pilot, visibly hung over but still cheerful, was studying a map as he arrived. Curious, Larsen looked at it over his shoulder. Never before, he thought, had he seen a chart so devoid of man-made features. No towns, no villages, no roads, no railways, only a scrambling of mountains interlaced with the wandering blue ribbons of countless rivers, with here and there a few isolated lakes. To the north lay an unmarked expanse of tundra slashed by the sweeping scimitar-curved scar of the Colville river.

'Here's where we're heading,' said Tibbett, pointing with his cigar to a dot on the map Larson had not noticed so far. 'Anaktuvuk Pass. No great architectural splendours I'm afraid. Just a collection of prefabricated houses and shacks dropped haphazard in the snow, and a winter trail that leads nowhere. There's no other settlement for miles, so we can't miss it, and if we do we're bound to hit the new service road to Prudhoe Bay. It's not marked here. I keep meaning to draw it in, but hell, everyone knows it's there.' He let fall a shower of ash over the map and swept it aside. 'Down here is the territory marked out for the Noatak reserve. Wild country, and further east it's even wilder. The Brooks Range, designated as the Gates of the Arctic National Park.'

'We flying over that?' asked Larsen incredulously.

'Hell no,' said Tibbett. 'We stay up here, over the foothills of the north slope. Still, you should get a good view of the mountains to the south.'

'Visual Flying Regulations?' queried Larsen.

'Pretty well. This old rust bucket doesn't rate anything very sophisticated in the way of electronics, and anyway half of them are no use out here. Still, I've flown the route a time or two, so I'm getting to know it now.' He folded the map and stowed it into a pocket on the door of the Cessna.

Larsen went to load his holdall in the luggage compartment behind the passenger seats, only to find the space almost filled by two large cardboard cartons. 'Freight,' explained the Texan. 'You're lucky, it could have been a team of huskies.' He glanced at his watch, then shrugged. 'Chief Umiak should be here any minute. He may be on time, but then again he might not. Time means nothing to these people.'

'Is he a chief?' queried Larsen.

'Hell, I wouldn't know. He skippers a whaleboat. Gives him some sort of social standing with his kinfolk, though hereabouts they only hunt whales in the spring. Rest of the year he works for the new native co-operative, looking after their land and money.'

Suddenly he laughed. 'Boy, you should've seen them in the bar last night after you'd gone to bed. Money! I tell you, we might as well have poured those millions down the drain, because that's where most of it is going.'

'If your government paid you compensation for land they had taken from you, I imagine you'd say it was nobody's goddamn business what you did with it.'

Neither man had heard Umiak approach. He stood there, neatly but warmly attired as though for a day's hunting, his trousers tucked into knee-length boots, a heavy wool jacket belted tightly over a blue shirt of the same material. On his head he wore a peaked cap with flaps which when pulled down, would serve as ear muffs. He carried a holdall in one hand and a gallon can in the other. He smiled almost apologetically as he spoke.

For a moment Tibbett flushed with embarrassment and anger, and then he relaxed. 'You're right, it's none of my goddamn business. After all, a lot of that money is coming my way.'

Without further comment, Umiak climbed aboard the Cessna, seating himself in one of the passenger seats behind the pilot. After a moment's hesitation Larsen joined him, leaving the Texan alone up front. The Cessna quivered and shook as the engine warmed to full power. Then they bounced and jolted along the airstrip, and took off into the sun.

Gradually the drone of the engine seemed to lessen as Larsen's ears adjusted to the sound. Below them the tundra stretched in a wide circle to the horizon, a bejewelled tapestry of fawns and browns, interwoven with threads of silver and crimson and gold, splashed with patches of muted green and olive. Small round ponds glistened like diamonds on cloth of gold, and here and there the land was patterned with giant hexagons fashioned by the frost. Always in attendance, small against the earth, lay the dense black shadow of the plane, like an albatross accompanying them into the unknown.

Slowly the land began to rise, rippling and humping away to the south, and in the valleys forgotten snow lay in grey-white drifts, draining away into silver tongues of streams that flashed briefly in the light and were gone. Umiak seemed wholly engrossed in the scene, shifting occasionally in his seat as some detail of the terrain caught his eye. Once he tapped Larsen on the knee and, pointing excitedly, said, 'Caribou.' Larsen stared down in the direction Umiak indicated, but he could discern nothing moving on the ground.

The plane was climbing now, gaining height as the ground rose beneath them. Snowfields were more numerous and wider in area, so that Larsen had to shield his eyes from the reflected glare of the sun, as to his right the mountains were rising like a wall

Individual peaks began to show, black against the sky, some serrated like shark's teeth, others curved in the menacing form of wolf's fangs. The ride grew bumpier, and Larsen felt his ears pop as the plane climbed even higher. The mountains were more broken now, with peaks rising to the north as well as the south, and from time to time they crossed wide valleys where rivers twisted in torment among the rocks and gravel bars which told of earlier floods. To the north the sky was blue, but to the east and south it was paler, whiter, and the far tops of the mountains were lost in haze. Suddenly Larsen noticed that the shadow of the plane no longer held stationary below them and, looking over his shoulder, saw that the sun had vanished from view.

Slowly but steadily the sky darkened. The mountains seemed to claw skywards, so that for a moment Larsen wondered if the plane was falling. The storm hit them, wrapped them in a veil of darkness, and snowflakes whirled and danced all around, spattering in star shells over the windscreen of the plane. Umiak leant forward, shouting to the pilot to turn north and fly out of it, but the Texan only shook his head, grinning, and pointed upwards. The first flash of lightning split the air, and the plane shook as though buffeted by a giant wing as the thundercrack drowned the roar of the engine.

The storm was but a local disturbance, a brief moment of exuberance in the riotous play of the elements among the jagged peaks and summits of the mountains. One of many thousand such events that tended to pass unnoticed by man, to go unrecorded on any weather map or chart. A sudden rise in the temperature of the air trapped in a deserted valley, a fall in barometric pressure, a wind eddying out of an unnamed abyss, any one or more of these factors could spawn such a storm, which might die in infancy, or grow into a monster that could rage for hours, or even days.

Now hailstones added to the din, and as the Cessna began to climb hurricane-force winds, wild outriders of the storm, swept the little plane south. The hailstorm came thicker, together with slushy wet snow sweeping in like waves whipped from a stormy sea, breaking over the plane and pounding it with hammer-like blows. Now ice began to gather on the leading edges of the wings, its weight forcing the plane down, only to flake away again in great ragged chunks, causing the Cessna to leap once more skywards.

Grimly the pilot wrestled with the controls, cursing out loud as the plane bucked and lurched, a plaything of the storm. Behind him Umiak sat quite still, his head bowed, his face expressionless, only his clenched fists betraying his anxiety. Wildly Larsen looked about him. They were deep in the mountains now, and as he watched he saw through a rent in the clouds the gigantic black wall of a precipice rearing up beside them, so close it seemed he could reach out and touch it. Instinctively he flung up an arm to protect himself, but then the plane leaped skywards and as he was forced back in his seat Larsen saw the mountain peak flash past the window and fall below them.

Suddenly he remembered reading, among some national park regulations, the procedure to be followed for downed aircraft. At the time he had dismissed the matter as a typical example of bureaucratic overkill, an undue concern over an event unlikely to happen. On enquiry, however, he had learned that on average four planes crashed in Alaska every week. Now it was about to happen to him, and strangely, he felt no fear, only a deep regret that his life was about to end, senselessly, uselessly, with so many ambitions left unfulfilled. If I have to die, he thought bitterly, why can't it be for some purpose?

Then, as if in answer to his unspoken prayer the storm began to abate. The snow and hail turned to rain, the clouds began to whiten, and the lightning now flickered away behind them. Gradually the rain lessened to give way to a white cotton-wool mist, and all three men began to relax. Tibbett pointed away to his left. 'Guess we maybe drifted a bit off course,' he shouted. 'I'm going to try and fly out of this. Take a look around.'

There was no warning, no premonition of danger ahead. Quite gently the Cessna slid on to the shoulder of a snow-covered hill, the rounded flank of an unnamed mountain on the northern slopes of the Brooks Range. It might have been a normal landing, and for a moment it seemed as though the pilot would succeed in bringing the plane to a halt. Then one wingtip clipped the side of the hill and the plane slewed sharply round. Even then all might have been well but for a buttress of granite, a ragged clenched fist of rock that had stood poised for centuries awaiting this, the exact moment to strike. The cabin was filled with the scream of tortured metal as the propeller bit vainly into the rock. The control panel buckled and heaved and the windscreen shattered. In the end the pilot proved himself a professional, for as he looked death in the face his last act was to cut the power to the engine, thus obviating the risk of fire. Then he looked away from death, and Larsen caught a last fleeting glimpse of the pilot's face, his eyes staring and his mouth open in a final despairing gasp, as the gauntlet of granite smashed into the top of his head, driving his skull deep into his brain. At that moment Larsen knew the pilot was dead. Then he too felt an inexorable force fling him forward, felt a violent blow to the side of his own head, and knew no more. The door of the plane burst open and a flurry of wind swept into the cabin, ice-laden, stinging with tiny particles of frozen snow. Then the full fury of the storm returned.

For a long time Joe Umiak sat silent, his eyes bright, his whole being intent and listening, seemingly alert for fresh dangers to come. It was, he thought, like the moment when the great whale lies still, when the danger and the risk of failure have passed, and when, despite the splash of waves on the boat and the shouts and chatter of the excited crew, you sit alone, in a circle of silence, wrapped in an aura of reflection and calm, before reality returns and the hard work of towing the carcase back to land begins.

Then he laughed softly to himself, a low throaty chuckle quite unlike the nervous giggle he was prone to when in the company of white men and ill at ease. The giggle was an affliction of which he was not proud, but which he had tried in vain to suppress. It was a legacy of his schooldays, of a time when even the threat of a beating failed to control the mirth that continually bubbled up inside him. It was a trait that had enabled his people to feel the joy of life, even among the most adverse conditions that the world has to offer. It was a survival mechanism, and one which generations of stern Presbyterian schoolteachers failed utterly to comprehend. Later he had learned that all white men tended to take work, and even life, seriously, and he had tried to emulate them, not always with success. Now he laughed, not because there was anything funny about his situation, but from the sheer joy of finding himself still alive.

The pilot was dead. Of that he had no doubt. He could see the man's skull caved in about his ears. Blood ran in untidy trickles down into the collar of his coat and the metallic reek of it mingled with the fumes of petrol, oil, and hot engine. He reached over and closed the door, for death still waited out there in the storm, and then he looked across at Larsen, slumped forward in his seat. He must have hit his head at the moment of impact, but though unconscious he was still alive. Umiak could hear him breathing, snoring like a man in a drunken stupor, his seat belt still holding him in position. He sat the man upright, frowning as he did so.

It was, in a way, a pity that he lived. An injured companion could be a handicap in a situation such as this, especially a white man, for it was well known that they were notoriously inept when it came to coping with hardship and cold, even when they were well. Umiak had no way of telling how badly this one was hurt. He would just have to wait and see, but if the man died, it would be easier.

He settled back to await the passing of the storm, but almost immediately a thought came to him. Scrambling forward he began to search, first in the cockpit and then, finding nothing, about the body of the pilot. Almost immediately his fingers closed on what he was seeking, the butt of a revolver stuck in the waistband of the dead man's pants. It was a poor weapon, a thirty-eight of inferior manufacture, but it was fully loaded, and at least the Texan had kept it cleaned and oiled. He hoped he would not need it, but its weight in the pocket of his jacket made him feel slightly more secure.

Once more he sat back in his seat to wait. The plane vibrated and shook with the force of the wind. The air was filled with flying snow, whipped off the mountainside and thrown in frozen particles against the plane. The temperature in the cabin dropped and Umiak curled himself small to conserve heat, though he knew, from the melting snowflakes that filtered through the broken windscreen, that it was not yet cold enough to freeze.

Beside him Larsen breathed easier, and by and by Umiak fell into a doze.

With a deep shuddering sigh Larsen came swimming back to consciousness. The plane trembled and shook around him and for a moment he thought they were still airborne. Then recollection came flooding back, and with it the shock of the giant rock splintering the windscreen and the knowledge that the pilot had met a sudden and violent death. He glanced across at Umiak slumped in his seat, his face turned away. He too appeared to be either unconscious or dead. At once he was seized with a feeling of helpless rage. The danger of his predicament as yet failed to dawn on him. All he knew was that just as he was looking forward to escape from this bleak and desolate land it had reached out and grasped him, holding him prisoner.

Then his anger passed as a throbbing pain bit deep into his skull. With it came a wave of nausea and a sudden realization that his bladder was uncomfortably full. He glanced out of the window at a white mass of mist, automatically reaching for the door on his side of the cabin. As he released the catch the wind tore it open, dragging him with it so that he half fell out of the plane, retching and fumbling frantically at his clothing. The wind almost blew him flat on his face, and he realized that what he thought was mist was in reality snow frozen to tiny particles and whipped against him with abrasive force by the searing wind. Purged, voided, he struggled to climb back into the plane, and strong hands helped pull him up.

He lay back in his seat, gasping, as Umiak secured the door and sat back, watching him with expressionless eyes. 'We're in trouble,' Umiak remarked. He said it almost absentmindedly as a man might speak who had forgotten his latch keys, or taken a wrong turn at a junction. 'You must have taken a knock,' he went on. 'You've been out quite a while.'

Larsen wiped his eyes and lips. After the vomiting and exposure to the wind he was shaking with cold. Umiak remembered seeing a vacuum flask in the cockpit of the plane. Luckily it had survived the crash, and was filled with hot coffee. He poured a cup and Larsen took it eagerly.

The coffee was harsh and black, but it stilled his shaking. He curled his hands around the cup, and then remembering offered it to Umiak. The man shook his head, and without further bidding Larsen drained the cup. 'Where are we?' he asked. Umiak merely shrugged. 'There is a map, isn't there? I was looking at it before we took off.'

Umiak pointed to the empty map pocket in the door of the plane. 'It was stuffed in there, but the door flew open when we crashed. The wind must have carried it away.'

For a moment panic seized Larsen. 'We've got to look for it.'

'In this?' queried Umiak, pointing outside. 'It could be twenty miles away by now, and torn to shreds among the rocks.'

Larsen sighed in despair. The anger gripped him once more. 'But don't you know where we are? Dammit, you live here.'

Umiak smiled patiently. 'Nobody lives here. Anyway, I live more than a hundred miles away on the coast. My people are of the sea not the mountains.'

Helplessly Larsen looked about him, at the crippled plane, the white wreaths of frozen vapour swirling outside, at the pilot sitting motionless in death. 'Then we're trapped. But we can't stop here. We've got to get out, get back to civilization. We've got to do something.' A thought struck him. 'They'll come looking for us, surely? As soon as we are missed, they'll send a plane or a helicopter.'

Umiak sighed. It was very much as he had feared. This

white man was like all the rest, impatient, feverish, desperate to do anything except the one thing that made sense, to wait, to do nothing, to conserve body energy until it was needed. 'Until this storm passes no one will come looking, and we cannot move. Better to rest, to sleep perhaps, until we see.'

'How long, for God's sake?' demanded Larsen.

'A few hours maybe. Perhaps a day or more.' Privately he thought it could be a week, but he felt it best not to say so.

Larsen subsided. It made sense to stay with the plane. It was more likely to be spotted from the air than a human figure, provided it didn't become buried in snow. They could make a fire, make smoke. There was no wood to burn, but they could use the upholstery of the plane, and the wiring. Burning plastic gave off thick black smoke. Suddenly he remembered his conversation with Tibbett earlier that morning. According to him Umiak was a person of some standing in the community. 'You're expected, aren't you, in Anaktuvuk? Won't you be missed?'

Umiak smiled, but his eyes were bleak. 'I'm not expected. I only decided to take the trip when I heard there was room on the plane. As for being missed!' He was about to laugh, but checked himself. 'There're lots of people will miss me. The Department of Fish and Game, the Bureau of Land Management, federal agencies. They'll miss me, but I imagine they'll all feel kind of relieved to know I'm no longer around to bother them any more.'

'And your own people?' persisted Larsen.

'Sometimes I think they too would prefer to be left alone to go their own way, rather than have me continually nagging and goading them to stand up for their rights.'

Despite his impatience, Larsen was tempted to laugh. The man was being as negative and apathetic as the very people he complained of, yet he was oblivious to the fact. Typical Stone Age mentality, he thought, then instantly chided himself, remembering the arrow-head in his pocket. The maker of that could have had no room in his philosophy for the concept of defeat. So what was the matter with this guy? Clearly he had been well educated, was even a politician of sorts. Where was his inventiveness and resource?

As if he had asked the question out loud Umiak answered him, voicing his earlier thoughts. 'Sometimes the hardest thing of all in an emergency is to do nothing.'

It was then that Larsen remembered the tape, the recorded message he had mailed to his assistant before leaving that morning. When he didn't show on time Sylvie would start telephoning around. She was a hustler that one. She'd get things moving, a few days would be all it would take, and they could survive that long. Thus assured, his thoughts turned elsewhere. 'What about him?' he demanded.

The body of the pilot still sat at the controls. He seemed to have settled deeper into his seat, as a man might who has merely fallen into a doze. 'He's dead,' said Umiak. 'Top of his skull must be stove down inside his collar.'

'I meant, what are we going to do with him?'

'Leave him where he is. He's blocking the draught.'

Larsen glanced sharply at Umiak, but the man seemed perfectly serious, and indeed Larsen could see that he spoke the sober truth. 'Besides,' Umiak went on, 'his weight is helping to hold the plane down. If we throw him out we could quite easily turn over in this wind.'

Larsen hadn't thought of that. For all they knew, they could be lodged very precariously indeed, perhaps even close to a sheer drop. Until they could view their surroundings there was no way of telling. 'Relax,' he told himself. 'Relax and wait, like the man says.'

His head ached. Umiak had already closed his eyes and curled back into his favourite foetal position. Larsen tried to do the same but his mind would not let him rest. Suddenly he remembered the boxes, the cartons loaded into the luggage compartment behind his seat. What was in them?

One felt light, the other heavy. Whatever was in them was bound to come in useful, or was it? He ripped open the lighter one first, hoping it was not cigarettes. He had given up smoking some years ago and the agony of his withdrawal was seared on his memory. He had no wish to start again. It was not cigarettes, it was popcorn, bag after bag of roasted popcorn. Larsen sighed. Just the thing for a baseball game, but with nothing else to eat he had a feeling he would get awful sick of popcorn. He opened the other carton, less optimistic this time.

'Freezer bags,' he exploded. 'What in hell would an Eskimo want with a thousand and one assorted freezer bags?'

Umiak opened one eye. His expression was pained. 'We found that when we left our hamburger steaks lying about in the snow the huskies ate them overnight.'

I asked for that, thought Larsen ruefully. Umiak had closed his eyes again. Without opening them he said softly, 'The word Eskimo is an insult to my people. It is a term applied by some uncouth forest Indians meaning eaters of raw meat. It is inaccurate and offensive, as it was meant to be. We are Inupiat, the people.'

Larsen's mind harked back to Umiak's outburst earlier that day, when he had admonished the pilot over the waste of native funds. This guy sure is touchy, he thought. Still, I'm stuck with him, so I guess for now I'll have to try to get along. Aloud he said, 'No offence meant. I'm people too.'

'No offence taken,' answered Umiak. 'I just thought you'd be interested to know.'

There was silence in the plane. Gradually the light faded as outside the wind continued to blow. Larsen pulled his coat tighter round him, folded his arms and closed his eyes. For a brief moment he was conscious of the rocking of the plane, and then he fell asleep.

3

Fire!

Larsen woke in panic. As a non-smoker he carried neither lighter nor matches. He could not recall seeing Umiak using tobacco, and he was filled with sudden terror that they might be stranded without the means of cooking or heating. Then he remembered that the pilot smoked cigars. He was sure to have the means of making fire about his person.

They so badly needed fire. He was cold, colder than he could ever remember. His fingers and toes were without feeling and his joints felt stiff. It was still night, and he could barely make out the huddled shape of Umiak beside him. Ahead the dead pilot still sat sentinel, and it was a moment or two before he realized that the plane was no longer rocking and shaking. The wind had dropped.

Forcing his fingers to uncurl, he rubbed at the frozen moisture that rimed the window, and peering out he could just discern a dim whiteness that might have been either snow or mist. By laying his cheek against the frosted pane and squinting up he could see a patch of sky, ablaze with a scattering of stars. He tried to read his watch but failed, so began to massage his arms and legs, trying to restore his circulation. Gradually he began to recover. He was hungry and thirsty and remembered that there was coffee left in the flask, but that, he knew, he must share with Umiak. He thought of waking the man, but on reflection felt that not only would it be unkind, but perhaps unwise.

So he passed the time exercising in his seat, flexing his muscles and manipulating his joints, and gradually he began to feel a little warmer. It was lucky for them, he thought, that the plane had not caught fire on landing, especially with so much fuel left in the tanks. Then he recalled how, in the jungle, where the all-pervading dampness made it impossible to light a fire, they had made small stoves out of ration tins filled with sand soaked with petrol. You had to be careful about lighting them, or you could lose your eyebrows, but once lit they burned steadily for quite a while.

Scheming thus, he became aware that the cabin of the plane was slowly filling with pale grey light. Dawn was breaking, and his joy was such that to his amazement he felt a lump come into his throat and his eyes brimmed with tears. Impatient with his own weakness he scrubbed his face, feeling the rasp of his unshaven cheeks and longing for the luxury of hot water and a shave. At least there was breakfast, of a sort, and reaching behind him he helped himself to a packet of popcorn.

'Have you ever tasted seal oil, Mr Larsen?'

Larsen jumped, and then grinned across at the dark eyes that solemnly regarded him. 'No. What's it like?'

'Do you enjoy a gin and Martini?'

Larsen groaned. 'My weakness.'

'What about raw fish?'

Visions of Lake Superior herring, marinated in white wine vinegar, with crunchy rings of onion, along with an ice-filled glass of gin and dry Martini filled his mind. He could almost feel the drink bite his throat as it slid down and his mouth watered at the thought.

'You might care to try some.' Umiak busied himself in the baggage compartment behind the seats. He took one of the freezer bags, emptied a packet of popcorn into it, and decanted a couple of ounces of liquid from the gallon can he had stowed there.

'This is special,' he announced. 'It was to have been a gift for a friend of mine in Anaktuvuk, where products of the sea are rare and greatly prized. Our need though is greater than his. It is made from the oil of the *oogruk*, the bearded seal, which is best, and flavoured with *quogak*, a kind of sorrel.' He shook the bag so that the popcorns were liberally soaked with oil. 'Here, try,' he said. 'But be careful, it is strong.'

It was. When Larsen had finished coughing he found Umiak studying him anxiously, awaiting his approval. It was not, after all, so disagreeable. It was at once hot and sour, with overtones of fish. The oily feel in his throat afterwards was perhaps the most disagreeable aspect of the experience, and for a moment Larsen thought he was going to disgrace himself and retch. Then the sensation of nausea passed and he accepted some more. In a surprisingly short time he felt satiated and full, and left Umiak to finish the remainder of the bag.

'Now we must drink,' said Umiak.

The coffee was barely warm, and there was less than a cup each, but it cleansed the film of oil from Larsen's tongue and throat. 'If only we had more oil,' mused Umiak. 'I could make a lamp.'

Larsen told him about his idea for a stove, and Umiak listened, his eyes glittering with interest. 'We need a can of some sort.'

Larsen pointed to the gallon can containing the seal oil. For a moment Umiak looked crestfallen. Then he brightened. 'I can put the oil in a freezer bag. It will be safe there and then we can use the can.' He stood up. 'Meantime I have more urgent needs.' He opened the door and stepped out of the plane.

After a few moments Larsen followed. It was full daylight now, and he saw that they were imprisoned, almost entombed, in a narrow valley. Above them the mountains towered saw-toothed into the sky so that they had to crane their necks to see the peaks. The plane lay half buried in snow, as though it had tried to burrow away from the light and hide in the shadow of the hill.

Across the valley the slopes were bathed in sunlight, swept almost clear of snow by the wind, and shining red and gold in the morning light. A tiny stream trickled across the valley floor, glistening between sparkling white bars of sand. Turning back to the plane Umiak emerged with the top of the vacuum flask. 'Come,' he said, making his way to the stream. 'We must drink.'

'Why?' queried Larsen, as Umiak pressed him to a second cup of icy water.

'You must drink plenty in the cold, because you don't sweat,' explained Umiak. 'And if you don't sweat all the salts that should pass through your skin have to go through your kidneys. So you overload them. A man can get in plenty of trouble that way.'

'Better if this stuff was a bit warmer,' grumbled Larsen, but he did as he was told. Already Umiak had deserted him and crossed the stream, clambering up the slope of the hill. Almost immediately he returned, his hand cupped in front of him.

'Fruits of the Arctic,' he announced, holding out his offering, half a dozen blueberries.

Larsen regarded them sourly. His breakfast still sat queasily on his stomach, in company with the water he had drunk. 'Those won't keep us going for long,' he remarked.

'They will if you eat enough of them,' retorted Umiak. 'My people pick hundreds of pounds every year, and store them for the winter. They are rich in vitamins and minerals, and the sugar stored in them will give you the energy to withstand the cold.'

Larsen, whose experience of berry picking was limited to the occasional expedition during his childhood, when a gallon pail was considered a sufficient harvest for the season, tried to visualize a hundred pounds of berries, and failed. 'I still don't think we're going to get fat on them.'

'Bears do,' said Umiak, and then he stood very still. The berries fell at his feet, and Larsen, watching him, saw fear flicker in his eyes. 'Bears do,' he repeated softly, staring up towards the head of the valley.

Then a tentacle of fear reached out and gripped Larsen too. This, he knew, was bear country, the last stronghold of the grizzly bear, perhaps the most dangerous quadruped in the whole of the Americas, and they were alone and unarmed. 'Do you think... Is it likely that there are bears around here?' he asked.

Umiak shrugged, hesitated and then shook his head with more conviction than he felt. 'Unlikely,' he said. 'We're probably too high up in the mountains, and anyway soon the bears will be denning up for the winter.'

Thoughts of winter brought a fresh tremor of fear to Larsen. 'I've been thinking,' he said, anxious to change the subject. 'The way the plane is, it's going to be in deep shadow all the day. If we could manhandle it down here it would be warmer. Also it would be more noticeable from the air. We could weight it down with boulders, in case there's another storm.'

Umiak nodded. 'First, though, we must deal with the pilot.'

Together, one pushing, the other pulling, they manhandled the corpse out of the plane. It lay on its back in the snow, grotesque and yet ludicrous, the limbs stiffened in death so that the legs and arms stuck up in the air. Umiak pressed down on the feet and the body slowly sat upright, allowing him to search the pockets. Almost at once Umiak found the lighter and held it up in triumph. Larsen felt a wave of relief so great that his knees trembled. 'You've been thinking about that, too?' he queried.

Umiak nodded and went on searching, but there was little more of any use to them. A wallet, some change, a cigar case and keys – Umiak bundled them in the dead man's handkerchief and set them to one side. Then, almost before Larsen realized what he was about, Umiak began to strip the corpse of its clothing. Without thinking Larsen reached out to stop him.

Umiak spun round as if he were about to be attacked, his face pale with anger. He crouched in the snow as though ready to spring, and then suddenly he relaxed. 'I thought,' he said, 'that since our friend is not likely to feel the cold any more, we would have more use for his clothing.'

'It's too small for either of us,' demurred Larsen. 'He was only a little guy.'

Umiak sighed. 'Take off his pants,' he explained patiently, 'split them down the crutch, and you've got a pair of leggings. The sleeves of his coat and shirt will make mitts, wrist warmers, and so on. You were cold last night, weren't you? You are going to get even colder. We're going to need all the insulation we can get.'

Naked, the corpse seemed somehow less human. Dragging it by the heels they hauled it across the snow to a site where the ground was littered with loose boulders. They found a niche between three large rocks and, bundling the body in, they began to pile loose stones over and around it.

They worked in haste, as if anxious to hide the evidence of a crime, each man silent, preoccupied with his own thoughts. Umiak was thinking of the Wendigo. Far to the south, where dense forest covered the land, the natives had a belief that if a man lingered too long in the woods he would become possessed by an evil spirit, one which would drive him mad and make him turn cannibal. In truth the forest inhibited life. The trees shut out light, so there was no grazing for game, and a hunting party lost or stranded in the woods could easily starve. The thoughts of hungry men might turn to cannibalism as a way of survival, and since this would be a crime against humanity the people absolved themselves from guilt by their belief in the Wendigo. No man possessed by an evil spirit could be held responsible for his actions. How long, Umiak wondered, would it be before the spirit of the Wendigo entered one or other of their souls, especially if they were trapped in this valley for any length of time?

Larsen likewise was thinking of the body of the dead pilot in terms of a supply of meat. It would not be the first time in the history of the United States that survivors of a disaster had kept themselves alive by cannibalism. The grim saga of the Donner family, stranded in the Rocky Mountains, was well documented, and Bill (Cannibal) Williams, the mountain man, had survived six weeks in a blizzard by eating the flesh of his companion, an Indian squaw. Then there was the case of Packer, who had helped to eat five of his companions. There had been other, more recent incidents reported following plane crashes in the wilderness.

Larsen was no stranger to death, and in his time had been witness to far more gruesome sights. In the tropics the body would have begun to decompose by now, be bloated and swollen and ripe with the sweet sickly smell of decay. Up here in the cold the body would keep for weeks, though Larsen knew that already the inexorable process of decay had begun. There was the familiar scent of blood, rusty and metallic, though here no flies came to lay their eggs in the crushed skull or explore the body orifices. Perhaps, thought Larsen, they ought to hold some sort of funeral service, if only as a form of insurance against them disinterring the body at a later date. On a more practical level, it might be advisable to disembowel the corpse, with a view to preserving the meat.

His mind flashed back to his boyhood, and the

butchering of his first deer. They had strung the doe up by her hind legs to the branch of a tree. He had heard the sharp inrush of air as the knife entered the abdomen, and had watched in stunned disbelief as the intestines cascaded out, coil after seemingly endless coil, to lie in glistening heaps in the bloodstained snow.

Rough granite rock slithered over greasy cold skin that yielded to its weight. Suddenly Larsen's stomach revolted at the thought of eating human flesh and he turned aside, vomiting. Umiak worked on in silence, choosing the heaviest rocks he could find. Though not noticeable to human nostrils, the smell of death, he knew, was already being signalled across the wilderness, attracting the attention of any carnivore, glutton or wolf or bear, that might be hunting nearby. Meantime he was not too displeased at this sign of squeamishness on the part of the white man. One thing could lead to another, and once a man adapted to the idea of cannibalism, it was but a short step from eating one who had already died to an appraisal of those comrades still living.

Later Larsen sat on a rock in the sun. The stream had risen slightly as the warmth of the day melted the snow on the mountain slopes, but it was still little more than a trickle among the stones. By damming the stream and scooping out the sand and gravel behind the dam Larsen was able to create a pool deep enough to wash in.

Earlier they had manhandled the plane out of the shadows and down the mountain slope to a flat hummock of ground beside the stream. The starboard wing had fractured on impact with the hillside. During the night the wind and the weight of driven snow had completed the break, and now it lay where it had parted from the plane, halfway down the slope. They had anchored the Cessna by piling boulders around the wheels and against the tailplane, and patched the hole in the windscreen with freezer bags, stuck down with the best part of a roll of sealing tape supplied with the bags.

It would not hold in a gale, but it was better than nothing. By the time they were finished Larsen was sweating under the sun, though the moment he stepped back into the shadow of the hill the air struck chill as a tomb. Now, with Umiak away across the valley picking berries, he took time to bathe in the icy water, partly to refresh himself, partly to rid himself of a feeling of contamination, the taint of death. He had finished dressing, and was pulling on his shoes and socks when Umiak returned.

The berries were fat and round, bursting with juice, but Umiak had not, it seemed, been finicky in his choice of fruit. Some were withered and dry. There were bits of leaf and twig mixed among them, and small crushed and injured insects struggled among the berries. Umiak divided his harvest into two equal piles and began to eat, grinning as he watched Larsen pick out the debris. 'I thought Americans liked a salad on the side,' he teased. 'Eat – leaves, bugs, berries, it's all food.'

Larsen was hungry. He had lost his breakfast in the snow. So he did as he was told, and found the rich flavour of the berries masked any other taste. 'Pity the stream isn't a bit bigger,' he remarked idly. 'I could have had a go with my fishing rod.'

Umiak stopped eating. For a moment he stared intently at Larsen, wondering if this was a sample of American humour. Larsen chewed on, his blue eyes guileless, his features empty of deceit. 'You have your fishing tackle with you?' Umiak asked quietly.

Larsen nodded. 'I always carry a few bits and pieces with me, on the off chance that I might get a bit of sport. It's not much. A little telescopic rod, that just fits in my holdall, a few flies, lures, and assorted hooks. It's not a lot of use up here, though.'

Umiak finished the last of his berries. 'May I see this fishing tackle please?'

Larsen went to the plane and came back with his rod

and reel, and two tobacco boxes filled with an assortment of lures, flies, sinkers, hooks and swivels. Umiak ignored the rod, but tested the strength of the monofilament nylon line, and picked out half a dozen of the smallest hooks. 'May I use these?' he queried.

'Sure,' said Larsen, intrigued.

Swiftly Umiak stripped line off the reel, cutting it with his teeth into lengths about two feet long. To each length he tied a hook, and then, as an afterthought, cut several longer lengths of line. Gathering them together he set off without a word across the valley to the berry patch. Larsen followed, his curiosity now fully roused.

The berries still clung thickly to the low, wind-bitten bushes. Here and there a cluster of fruit riper and juicier than the rest clung invitingly to the stem, and choosing his berries with care Umiak inserted a hook into the fruit, tying the other end of the nylon to a stout branch. When he had used up all his hooks he fashioned snares from the longer lengths of nylon, attaching one end to the twisted roots of the shrubs, and spreading the snares flat in the thin powdering of snow that covered the thick moss growing at the base of the bushes.

Larsen watched in silence. Finally, still kneeling, Umiak tugged at his trouser leg and pointed to the ground, at something Larsen had not noticed before. It was a dropping, though from an animal or bird he could not tell. It lay curled like a worm casting, neatly coiled in a small pyramid. Further on he saw another one, and then, as his eyes grew accustomed to finding them, he saw the ground below the bushes was liberally sprinkled with them.

'Ptarmigan,' explained Umiak. 'They must come here regularly to feed on the berries. Hopefully we'll get one or two.' He paused to make minute adjustments to a couple of the snares. 'The trick is to get the snare slightly larger than their feet. Too small, and their feet won't go through. Too big, and they'll step right in and out again.'

'When will they come?' queried Larsen.

'Tonight, tomorrow, who knows?' said Umiak. 'They'll come, though, as long as there are berries left.'

They set off back to the plane. On the way Umiak asked, 'Have you any more surprises in your bag, Mr Larsen?'

Suddenly Larsen remembered his knife. It was the sort of penknife beloved of small boys, no more than a toy, an intricate maze of folding blades and gadgets, all wholly impractical but delightfully ingenious. His mother had given it to him when he joined the marines, and rather than hurt her feelings he had carried it with him.

He had never done more with it than peel the occasional apple, but since her death he had always kept it about him as a sort of memento. Reluctantly, and with a faint feeling of embarrassment, he produced it for Umiak's inspection.

He had expected ridicule. Instead Umiak's attitude was one almost approaching reverence. For a while he stared at it intently, and then began a prolonged and meticulous examination, testing every blade and gadget, opening and closing each one several times, but always with extreme care. He reminded Larsen exactly of a small boy presented with a gift, and then he remembered the arrow-head, and it occurred to him that Umiak was descended from a race of men obsessed with miniaturization. All at once he was filled with an irrational fear that Umiak would want to keep the knife, and he half held out his hand for its return, only to withdraw it again in confusion.

Umiak caught the gesture, and almost wistfully handed it back. 'An anthropologist once remarked to me that he thought my people were "unnecessarily gadget burdened". There is perhaps an element of truth in what he said, but then we are not stupid, and for centuries we have sought to improve our technology, to seek more sophisticated ways of capturing the game on which our lives depend. So, what more natural, during the long dark days of winter, when hunting is an impossibility, than for a hunter to pass the hours of idleness designing more efficient weapons. When I see something like that knife, I wonder what my people might have invented, given the necessary raw materials with which to work? Not a Swiss watch perhaps. We would have no use for such a thing. But a knife like that . . . ?'

He let the query trail away, feeling he had been guilty of undue boasting. Instead he smiled and shrugged apologetically.

'Talking of Swiss watches,' said Larsen, 'your people also seemed to have had a passion for working in miniature.' For a moment he hesitated, fingering the arrow-head in his pocket. Strictly speaking he knew that his possession of it was illegal. Furthermore, he was not sure how Umiak would react to his looting of an archaeological site, albeit on a very miniature scale. Under the circumstances it seemed a matter of very small importance, so he drew it out and passed it to Umiak.

Umiak glanced at him slyly, and Larsen guessed what he was thinking. 'My people find many of these,' he remarked, testing the point of the arrow on his thumb. 'We knew about them long before the archaeologists from the universities of California and Alaska came digging. In fact a legend grew up, and still persists, a belief that our ancestors were very small people. Yet there were many reasons for working with small objects. Shortage of raw materials was one. The only wood we had was that washed up from the sea. Wood was to us like gold to you. Bows were made of wood or whalebone. Small bows fired small arrows, and small arrow-heads pierced thick hide better than large heavy ones. It was easier and quicker to drill a hole through a small piece of bone or stone than to drill a large piece. Small weapons were lighter to carry for nomads who went everywhere on foot. Lack of fuel, save seal oil, meant small lamps. Small homes were easier to keep warm, and so on.'

He passed the arrow-head back to Larsen. 'Take care of it, Mr Larsen. It was made with care. And take care of that beautiful knife of yours. We may well have need of it.'

In fact they found a use for it straightaway, converting the gallon can into a petrol stove. Together they designed it, cutting a flap of metal from one side of the can, but leaving it hinged to act as a windshield, or perhaps, they hoped, a hotplate. They had some trouble draining petrol from the fuel tank of the plane, and wasted quite a bit, but at last they had about half a gallon in one of the plastic bags. The fire burned well, but to Larsen's chagrin with a sooty black flame.

'It's the residue of seal oil in the can,' explained Umiak. 'It always smokes. Soon it will clear. A hot drink would be nice,' he added.

Larsen, who had been trying not to let his mind dwell on thoughts of scalding coffee, felt a wave of irritation. 'What can I offer you?' he asked sarcastically.

'Water,' said Umiak. 'There's nothing else.'

'And nothing to boil it in,' pointed out Larsen.

Umiak sighed and sat silent for a while. Then he got up and began pottering among the stones. Larsen, disinterested, sat on alone, hunched over the flames of the stove, straining his ears in the silence in the hope of hearing a plane, for already he was growing to dread the thought of another night of discomfort and cold. There was nothing, no sound save that of Umiak clattering among the rocks. The valley was devoid of life, and not even a raven showed in the sky above the crags.

His reverie was interrupted by Umiak, who appeared at his side with a handful of round flat pebbles, which he proceeded to pile on the stove. Then he squatted back on his heels, watching the flames play over the stones. Nearby he had built a nest of rocks and moss, lining it with a plastic bag which he had half filled with water. When he judged the pebbles hot enough he deftly shovelled them out of the flames, using two flat slates he had chosen for the purpose. Swiftly he transferred them to the water, which hissed and bubbled as the stones sank. In a few moments the water was too hot to touch.

Umiak dipped the cup in the water and offered it to Larsen. The brew did not look inviting. The stones had blackened with carbon from the residue of the seal oil and bits of it floated on the surface of the cup. Larsen shook his head and without comment Umiak withdrew his offer and drank.

Larsen watched, angry and impatient that all this thought and endeavour should go to producing a mere cup of dirty water, without even the value of nutrition. Umiak drained the cup.

'You should have some,' he insisted. 'Better to drink hot water than cold. You drink cold water, you burn energy heating it inside you, energy you can't afford to lose.'

Larsen was not tempted however. He was tired of lessons in survival, and ill disposed to listen to lectures on the subject. Sensing this Umiak sat silent, but secretly he longed for the company of his own people, with their Rabelaisian humour and heavy-handed wit. This white man depressed him.

Abruptly he got up and wandered away down the valley, following the course of the stream as it wound its secret way, half hidden by tussocks of reeds and moss between the stones that littered the valley floor. To his right the snow-clad mountains lay in deep shadow. To his left the sun bronzed the tawny hide of the hill, with its darker mane of berry bushes, here and there auburn with the first touch of winter. Snow lay in broad scattered drifts, sculpted by the wind into strange shapes that etched blue-black shadows on a background of sparkling white.

For the stream there was a way out of the valley, but there was no guarantee that a man might follow. At any point the valley floor could terminate in a sheer drop that would be impossible to negotiate, in which case it would be necessary to seek an alternative route out. In which direction that might lie he could not begin to guess.

The grandeur of the scene was not lost on him. Neither was it alien to him, for some years ago he had hunted regularly in these mountains, though further away to the east. Alone he knew he could survive. Of that he was deeply, quietly assured, and this knowledge blended with an instinctive love of the land of which he felt so much a part left him with no room in his mind for fear or concern.

The presence of the white man did, though. There was a difference between the two races, in their attitude to the world about them, and over the years Umiak had come to identify the cause. For ten thousand years his people had learned to live with the land, to adapt to the seasons and the weather, and to learn to make the best use of all that the world had to offer. At some point during that time the white men, the strangers, had grown dissatisfied with their lot, and in so doing had lost the ability to survive as part of the natural world. They had failed to adapt their ways to natural cycles, and instead had evolved ways to survive in what slowly became, for them, an alien world. First they had learned to domesticate stock. Then they had gone on to cultivate crops. From that point on they had been compelled more and more to fight against the forces of the wild, until now it was as if their civilization had become a sort of spaceship from which they dared venture out only for short periods to view an alien planet. Once deprived of their life support systems they could not long survive.

In the days to come Larsen would grow to need him. The man was not yet prepared to accept this, though, and

Umiak was not sure how to convince him without antagonizing him. On the other hand, he did not need Larsen. Almost without conscious thought, his hand stole to the butt of the pistol concealed in his pocket.

It would be so easy. All he had to do was to walk up behind the man and shoot him in the back of the head. Larsen would die quite suddenly, without pain, without fear, without the slightest prescience that his end had come. It would be kind in a way, kinder than simply abandoning him to his fate, kinder even than letting him run the risk of suffering from cold and hunger and the danger of frostbite. One shot would free him for ever from this land he called a wilderness which he appeared to hate and fear so much.

Yet even as he considered the prospect he knew it would be too easy. All his life he had worked for a better understanding between his people and the white strangers, striving, in spite of a fundamental difference in outlook, to achieve an acceptable blend of both their cultures. Now here he was, faced with a small personal problem of his own, seeking to justify an easy way out, not, he had to admit, for Larsen, but for himself. He was forced to smile at his own duplicity. All the same, he mused, it might be wise to keep his options open.

Though his mind wandered his eyes were busy, scanning the ground at his feet in search of what, for want of a better term, he called 'sign'. There was little enough to be seen, a dried lozenge of fur and bone, the age-old casting of a snowy owl dried and preserved by the Arctic wind. He crossed the faint meandering trail that was possibly the path of a ground squirrel, and noted a few bitten heather shoots where ptarmigan had grazed. A shadow flickered across the sun, and gazing upwards he spied an eagle sailing on stiff outstretched wings. It circled once and was gone. There was nothing to attract it in this barren valley.

Larsen too saw the eagle. Its presence served only to

accentuate his plight. Master of the air, it could with a tilt of its wings ride one of the swift currents that swept over the mountain range. In an hour it could be twenty, thirty, fifty miles away. In a day, without effort, without hunger, without cold, it could cross a stretch of country it might take him a month to travel.

Umiak was now no more than a mere dot on the horizon, and as Larsen watched he disappeared into a fold of the landscape, the dead ground hiding him from view. Larsen recalled how often the tiny figures of the Vietcong had performed a similar disappearing trick. Only then they were advancing, and then would come the interminable wait, finger on trigger, not knowing how soon, or how close they would reappear. Uncanny how closely Umiak resembled a Vietnamese, but then he was retreating, he was out of range, and anyway he had no weapon. For the first time he regretted having given up sport hunting after he had left the army. If he had not, he might have had a rifle with him now, instead of a useless fishing rod. Not, he had to admit, that there was any game to shoot.

With Umiak gone the silence was profound. He could hear his own breathing, and the steady beat of his heart. Almost, he felt he could hear the blood coursing through his veins. He threw a stone to break the silence, and it clattered eerily among the rocks. The mountains threw back the sound, hollow, lifeless and mocking.

Time passed, and Umiak did not return. Where had the stupid bastard gone? Perhaps he had met with an accident, fallen over a cliff, or twisted his ankle on a loose stone. Perhaps a bear had got him. He recalled the sense of fear Umiak had betrayed at the earlier mention of them, and in spite of himself he looked around, his eyes probing the deep shadows of the hills, seeking any sign of movement.

As quickly as it had arisen, the small ripple of fear passed, as he chided himself for having given way to it.

Funny though, he thought, how the company of any fellow human, even one you didn't like, was more comforting that utter solitude. So where the hell was Umiak? Had he deserted him? He was tempted to call his name, but pride prevented him. All the same, it would do no harm to take a stroll, go and meet the guy. He had just risen to his feet when he heard the plane.

At first he thought his ears were deceiving him, the drone was so faint. Then he heard it again, louder, unmistakable this time. He looked up, but the sky was empty. The plane was somewhere beyond the mountains. Unless it flew directly overhead it would miss them, and perhaps not return. Somehow he had to attract attention, and the only way was with smoke.

He ran to the Cessna, cursing himself for not preparing a fire earlier. Frantically he searched for something to burn. The rear seats were detachable in order to make more room for cargo, but he had no time to struggle with them. His hand fell on the dead pilot's jacket and he hurried away with that, anxious not to start a blaze near the aircraft. There was some petrol left in the plastic bag and he threw that over the coat before flicking the lighter.

The fumes ignited in an explosion of flame that scorched the side of his face, burning fiercely but giving off little smoke. The drone of the plane grew fainter, fading into the distance, but just as he was beginning to despair the sound of the engine gradually grew louder again. The plane was turning, still searching.

Seal oil smoked, and Umiak had a bagful. Larsen ran again to the plane, seized the container, and sprinkled the contents over the fire. The seal oil sputtered and fizzed at first, partly dousing the flames, but then itself beginning to burn with a yellow flame that gave off a dense sooty vapour. The column of smoke rose steadily into the air, oily and black. High into the sky above the valley floor it climbed, between the twin walls of the mountains, forty, fifty, sixty feet, and then, to Larsen's horror and dismay, it stopped rising, levelling off into a flat pall halfway up the mountainside. There it lingered, pancaking out and drifting across the valley as the warm rising air met the impenetrable barrier of the dense cold air of the mountain tops.

There was nothing he could do, only curse out loud in a desperate attempt to allay the fear that gripped him. At his feet the fire still smouldered, and savagely he kicked out at it. Part of one sleeve flared briefly to flame, wrapping itself and its coating of blazing seal oil round his leg, igniting his trousers and searing his leg with liquid fire.

Frantically he leaped away, but the jacket clung tenaciously to his leg, flames and smoke belching higher as in his attempts to free himself he fanned the blaze. For one wild moment he contemplated running down to the stream, but the life-saving water was too far away. In blind panic now he shook his leg, and mercifully the jacket fell away. Still the cloth of his trousers smouldered on, and only then did it occur to him to smother the fire with snow. Hopping around on one leg, he scooped up great handfuls, soaking the material until the last spark was extinguished. Then he stood, sobbing with relief yet too fearful to inspect the full extent of his burns. Only then did he become aware of the silence. The plane had gone.

4

Sheep droppings lay among the short wiry stems of the grasses. They were ancient and weathered and Umiak paid them scant attention. Sheep, like the stream, could go where no man might follow, and their presence here in the valley was no assurance of an easy way out. He looked away downstream. Somewhere amid the bewilderment of jagged peaks, some dark and foreboding, others splashed and whitened with snow, there had to be a way out, and the river alone knew. By now he had wandered a long way from the plane, but he decided to go just a little further.

Then, a few hundred yards downstream, he found the wolf scat, shrivelled and wind-dried, but hoary with sheep's wool and with here and there a fragment of bone. Then he knew that the way out was sure, and feeling lighter at heart he turned back to the plane. He still nursed a faint hope that he might come across the lost map, though he knew the chances were slim. As he gazed around he heard the sound of the engine.

His first impulse was to run back towards the Cessna, but then he checked himself and listened. The sound came from the north, far beyond the mountain peaks. The noise rose and fell, not intermittently as it might if borne on the breeze, but in slow regular intervals. The plane was circling, no doubt searching for them, perhaps in the area where they should have been had the storm not blown them off course. Then, as he listened, the drone faded and died, and then there was no sound save the gentle murmur of the brook as it trickled by at his feet.

It was after all most unlikely that the plane was searching for them. Even if the pilot had had time to send out any distress call, it was extremely improbable that it would have been heard. No one in the outside world knew where or why they had crashed. To find them the rescue services would have to search a corridor some thirty miles wide and three hundred miles long, over a tapestry of tundra and muskeg swamp, river and lake and poplar thicket spread amidst a maze of mountain peaks and unnamed hidden valleys.

They would check the obvious sites where a plane in difficulties might touch down. They would search the lakes, the gravel bars, the odd airstrip constructed by prospectors. They would ask others flying over the region to keep an eye open for wreckage, but beyond that there was little they could do. Missing planes were found, but sometimes only after months, or years. Many had disappeared, never to be located again.

It was possible that the plane he had heard had been searching for them. It was equally possible that it had been chartered by some of his own people, hunting for caribou, for now was the time when the great herds of deer began their winter migration south. It might have been a biologist doing a wolf count, or a white sport hunter looking for a bear. The reasons for a plane circling in the vicinity were many.

He came to a decision then. The resources of the valley in which they lay could not sustain them for long, and for Larsen and him there was only one way out, on foot, before starvation and winter cold destroyed them.

As he topped the ridge these thoughts were forgotten at the sight that met his eyes. A fire smouldered on the ground, and Larsen was indulging in what appeared to be a comic travesty of an Indian war dance, hopping and leaping and slapping at his leg. Then, as Umiak drew nearer, the truth began to dawn on him.

Half angry, half ashamed, Larsen explained what had happened. Umiak listened, his face a mask. At first he could not believe that anyone would be so stupid as to waste nearly a gallon of precious seal oil just to make smoke. Then anger overtook him as he realized that the man had thrown away what was perhaps their only hope of survival in the days to come. For a moment he was tempted to kill him on the spot and leave his body to the ravens and the wolves.

Then he began to laugh. He was, after all, a child of adversity, and this was the sort of misfortune that he and his kind had laughed at since the dawn of time. If a man fell through the ice, if a sled overturned, if a man shot himself in the foot, it was an occasion not for grief, but for mirth. Now the thought of a man setting his own trousers on fire struck him as so funny that he laughed until the tears came to his eyes. If he survived, it would be a story to tell over and over again to his people, and the thought sent him again into a fresh paroxsym of mirth.

Bewildered and angry, humiliated at being made the butt of Umiak's childish sense of humour, Larsen limped moodily down to the stream and began to bathe his leg. The ice-cold water soothed it, and was perhaps the best treatment he could apply under the circumstances. One burn was severe, and though it was not crippling it was, as luck would have it, exactly over the site of his old wound. The great danger, Larsen knew, was infection, even in this cold climate. As with all burns, the wound at the moment was sterile, but the skin was destroyed, dead, and would eventually slough away. Beneath, sheltered from light and air, organisms would multiply and breed, eating into the tissues, and without antibiotics to combat them he had only the defences of his own body. Abscesses might develop. There was even the risk of gangrene. He was bandaging his leg with strips of cloth from a spare shirt he carried in his holdall when Umiak approached, bringing a wad of soft clean moss with which to pad the burn.

Larsen accepted it for what it was, a flag of truce, and was forced to admit to himself that it brought a measure of comfort. For a long while they sat without speaking, each man eager to break the silence, but reluctant to be the first. 'Where do you suppose we are?' asked Larsen at last.

'I've been trying to work it out,' replied Umiak. With his finger he drew a long sausage shape in a patch of melting snow and placed a dot at either end. 'This,' he said, pointing to the sausage, 'is the Brooks Range, a chain of mountains dividing the land in two. Now we left here,' he went on, pointing to the left-hand dot, 'to fly to here,' indicating the other dot. 'Flying time should have been about three hours, maybe a bit more in that old plane, and we'd been flying for about an hour and a half.'

'Which puts us smack in the middle of the mountains,' groaned Larsen.

'Not quite,' said Umiak. 'Not in the middle, on the edge. It's hard to tell down here in the valley, but I think we must be on the north slope. It's important, if we are to try and find our way out. North, there is nothing but open tundra. We would be walking into the coming winter, and if the wind was to blow we'd freeze to death in a matter of hours. To go south we'd have to cross the mountains, and though there are settlements along the rivers there, we might have a hard time finding them.'

'What about turning back?' queried Larsen.

Umiak shook his head. 'Again there would be miles of open tundra to cross. The only settlements are on the sea coast, and we have no way of knowing where they lie. There is a compass in the plane, if it still works, but without a map it is useless.'

'So we head east,' said Larsen. 'But it seems to me we're not a lot better off. We still have to traverse the mountain range and there's no guarantee we'll hit civilization even if we survive. How far is it? A hundred, two hundred miles? How long will it take us? A week? A month?'

Umiak sighed. So many questions. 'If we travel far enough, we're bound to reach the oil road that runs north to Prudhoe Bay. But it's not quite as simple as that. To walk in a straight line over the mountains is out of the question. The going would be too hazardous and rough.'

He began to draw again on his map. 'The rivers on this side of the mountains generally flow north, to join one great river. Other streams flow east and west out of the mountains. Let's suppose we follow this stream at our feet. When we find one joining it from the east, we follow that.

'A man is never quite lost as long as he has a stream to follow. Besides, there will be berries, game of some sort, shelter and perhaps firewood along the river banks. There may be fish to catch with that fishing rod of yours. The rivers will not freeze for a while yet.'

Umiak spoke sense. Larsen could see that, yet part of him still recoiled from the prospect. 'But it could take weeks, wandering about in the wilderness like that, and the longer it takes, the worse the weather is going to get. Wouldn't we be better off waiting here a while longer?'

As gently as he could, Umiak spelled out the unlikelihood of rescue. 'The wilderness has kept my people alive for ten thousand years,' he murmured. 'Perhaps it will protect us for a few weeks more. It is a good place to be, providing you obey the rules, and don't do anything foolish. Besides, a few years ago I hunted west out of Anaktuvuk Pass with the friend I was on my way to visit yesterday. I can't promise, but sooner or later we might come to a region I remember. Also, if we can find them there are odd cabins, and old camp sites used by my people on their hunting trips. Who knows, we might meet up with such a party on our way.'

Larsen sat a long while in silence. He desperately wanted to escape from this barren unyielding land, to relax in a hot bath and savour the warmth and comfort of a clean bed, to sink his teeth into a good steak and hear the tinkle of ice in a glass as he poured whisky over it. He wanted to hear the roar of traffic and feel a firm pavement under his feet. He wanted all these things he had dreamed about so longingly many years ago. He had prayed then that he might never again find himself in a similar situation, but his prayers had been denied. He desperately wanted to escape from the prison confines of this valley, but the way out, and the days of journeying ahead filled him with horror and dismay. This was no mere three-day jungle patrol, with a helicopter ride back to base to look forward to at the end. This was a journey perhaps without an end, except that of a slow death from starvation and cold. His frustration and anger turned on the lean olive-skinned figure of the man sitting in silent reflection beside him. 'If this goddamned wilderness is so special, such a good place to be, why aren't your own people living here?'

At first Umiak seemed reluctant to answer, and then he began softly to speak, hesitantly, as a man might recalling events long past, beyond belief and painful to recall. 'This land is great and my people were few, but for centuries they wandered the hills and river valleys. They followed the deer and fished the streams, they harvested the roots and berries and birds' eggs in their season. They knew where the bears dug their dens and the beaver built their lodges. Others lived near the sea and hunted the seal and the walrus and the whale. From time to time people would meet and trade caribou skins for whale oil, or exchange the skins of the bearded seal, which makes the best ropes and footwear, for the soft pelts of fox or lynx, or for meat which did not taste of the sea.

'Then the white men came. Whalers from the sea and fur traders journeying up the rivers. In return for our labour and meat and furs they offered us many things, whisky, tobacco, iron, cloth and guns. So the people came out of the country to settle near the rivers and the coast, near to the white men, so that they could enrich themselves with the goods the white men brought.

'Now it is true that we did not need these things. As long as we were in ignorance of the white men's riches, we did not hanker after them. After all, are we so very different from you? Before you invented the automobile and the television, you did not hanker after them, but once they came on the market everyone had to have one. So it was with us.

'The white men brought us other gifts, syphilis, smallpox, measles and tuberculosis. In return they robbed the land of its wealth, and when they no longer needed whalebone and furs they went away, leaving our people sick and starved. Then the missionaries came and told us we were suffering because we had sinned. But they also told us of a god, an all-powerful god who would forgive us our sins, if only we would learn the white man's ways. So the Bureau of Indian Affairs took our children away from us and boarded them in schools. They cut their hair short and dressed them in western-style clothing. Any child caught speaking its mother's tongue was severely punished. Instead they were taught to read and write and to speak only the white man's tongue.

'They taught them many things, but they did not teach them to fish and hunt, where to look for edible roots, or how to snare birds. Because our children were not allowed to be with their parents they could not learn these things. The girls did not know how to dress fish or tan hides. The boys did not know how to run on snowshoes and hunt the deer and hare. Above all, they did not learn to know the land, their land, the land that their fathers knew.

'So for a long time the people abandoned their land, and the ways that had served them so well. But we are wiser now, and while we appreciate much that the white man has to offer us, we have learned to value the old ways too, and we are relearning lost skills. The people of Anaktuvuk were among those who left the mountains for the sea. Twenty-five years ago they left the sea and returned to the hills. They are there still. Others might follow, but...'

Abruptly he stood up. 'The shadows grow longer and the night will be cold. I suggest we dismantle the seats in the plane, and with the carpet make ourselves a bed. It will be warmer if we share it. That is if you have no objection.'

They set to work with Larsen's little knife and the tool kit from the plane, ripping up the carpet and removing the upholstery from the seats to make a snug and comfortable couch. Glad of the activity and something to occupy his mind, Larsen felt his low spirits lifting a little. 'If we are going to sleep together, you'd better call me Steve,' he joked.

Umiak considered this solemnly. 'I don't think that would be at all appropriate,' he said finally.

'Suit yourself,' said Larsen, rebuffed. He was unable to decide whether to be insulted or amused. Maybe Umiak held him responsible for the suffering and privation brought on his people by the coming of the white man. The way he told it the tale was one of paradise lost, though privately he wondered if life had ever even remotely approached that of Eden. More likely the story was coloured with prejudice, tinged with guilt spawned from loss of innocence. Whatever, there was no way even Umiak could turn back the clock. On the other hand, maybe his formality was based on some cock-eyed legacy of the whaling days, when ships' officers always referred to each other as 'Mister'. Either way, it was not important.

As they worked the light rapidly began to fade. Clouds were gathering among the mountain tops, ragged veils of mist whipped into writhing torment by a bitter wind that came sweeping up the valley. Swiftly they descended, leaping from peak to jagged peak with alarming speed, sweeping down the mountainsides until the crags were hidden in dense black veils, that first condensed into icy squalls of rain and then rapidly turned to snow.

Larsen huddled with Umiak in the shelter of the cabin, stunned with awe at the sudden relentless savagery of the weather, as snow began to gather on the fuselage, a wet grey slush that rapidly whitened as the blizzard grew in intensity. This was just a taste of the conditions that sooner or later they would have to face, ill-equipped and ill-clad, without shelter of even the most rudimentary kind. He shivered, more with dread than cold.

Soon it grew almost too dark to see, and the valley was blotted out with swirling black flakes. Then, as abruptly as it had begun, the storm passed, and the night cold bit into their bones as the stars frosted the moonless sky.

5

It was extraordinary how much popcorn a man could eat without feeling satisfied. Larsen hoped it would not prove too binding a fare. He had enough problems as it was. Perhaps the berries, not to mention the leaves and bugs he had eaten, would help to counteract the effect.

At least he was comfortable, lying there in the dark, and almost warm under the carpet they had ripped from the floor of the plane. It smelled musty and foul, but at least Umiak didn't smell, lying there close to his side, his breathing soft and even. Larsen was not sure whether he was awake or asleep. Funny how formal and uptight he had been about the use of Christian names. He'd heard that Eskimos were inclined if anything to be over friendly, but he had not found it to be so. He'd even been told that at one time they used to share their wives with white travellers, and had often wondered if this had been true. For a moment he was tempted to ask Umiak, and then dismissed the idea. He had no wish for a further rebuff, and anyway under the circumstances locker-room talk, or should it be pillow talk, was definitely not to be encouraged.

Still, some of the Eskimo girls he had seen were remarkable for their beauty, and one at least had been prepared to be free with her favours, for a price. Feeling the heat rising within him, he banished the thought from his head, concentrating instead on a vision of an old Eskimo woman, fat-bellied, with withered sagging breasts, her breath reeking of fish and her mouth filled with rotten teeth.

From where he lay he could see the slope of the hill, dusted with freshly fallen snow and sparkling now with the reflected light of the stars. Outcrops of eroded rock bare of snow assumed strange shapes against the white. As he watched they seemed to swell and grow, then fade before his eyes. Strange how sometimes they seemed to move. He could have sworn just then that one drifted slowly across the hill.

Gradually he fell asleep, despite the pain of the burn in his leg. Once he woke, half dreaming, half imagining he had heard the clatter of stones in the night. All was still, silent save for the soft hiss of Umiak's breathing, and safe in the security of the cabin he drifted back to sleep.

The ptarmigan came with the dawn, before the men awoke. They settled in a flock near the berry patch, and then ran across to feed. They had almost completed their summer moult and only a few flecks of brown showed against their white plumage. First one and then another began to struggle helplessly as the hooks caught their throats and the nylon line held them fast. Alarmed, the rest of the flock took flight, all save one which rose on whirring wings, only to sprawl in the snow as the snare round its leg drew tight. Soon the hooked birds hung still, like great withered blossoms against a backcloth of green. Only the one on the ground continued to flap spasmodically from time to time, raising brief flurries of snow with its wings.

Larsen woke refreshed but hungry, and immediately his spirits fell at the thought of what lay in store for breakfast. The choice lay between frozen blueberries and popcorn, and neither prospect appealed. Then he remembered the traps Umiak had set. He looked out of the window of the plane and his shout brought Umiak awake. Together the two men fell out of the plane and raced across the snow. To his surprise Larsen found himself thinking that as an alternative to popcorn hot raw flesh was infinitely more appealing.

'We share,' said Umiak.

'Of course,' replied Larsen. 'Roast ptarmigan,' he murmured ecstatically.

'Soup,' corrected Umiak.

The two stopped and glared at each other. Umiak held the birds, and he had the air of a man who would not part with his prize easily. 'It's more nourishing, more economical...' he began.

'Look,' said Larsen. 'I'll do a deal with you. Let me roast one on the stones you will be heating for your soup, and you can have the other two. Umiak nodded, his face expressionless. He hefted the three birds in his hand, and gave the heaviest one to Larsen.

The meat was tough, and though the skin was charred black and crinkly the flesh near the bones was almost raw. Larsen had eaten his bird before Umiak had finished making his soup. Now he sat, sucking on the bones, still hungry, as Umiak began to fish portions of juicy meat from the freezer bag in which he had boiled them, washing them down with fragrant juice. He seemed to take an age over the meal, and the smell of the soup tormented Larsen almost beyond measure. Once he felt an overwhelming impulse to get up and walk away from temptation, but pride stopped him. He made up his mind that even if Umiak offered him a share he would refuse, but the man made no such gesture.

The shadows were shrinking now, the sun shedding a thin warmth as it lit the snow with rosy light. Larsen let his gaze wander over the valley, struck, in spite of his antipathy to his surroundings, by the stark sterile beauty of the scene. Then his jaw dropped. 'Oh my God,' he breathed. 'Oh sweet Jesus.'

Umiak looked up, and then stared in the direction

Larsen was pointing. The grave, the cairn of stones that covered the dead body of the pilot, had been broken into during the night, torn apart, and the stones hurled aside and scattered in the snow. Some of them, Larsen recalled, had been so heavy that it had taken their combined strength to manhandle them into place. From the grave a broad trail of beaten snow stretched away down the valley, to disappear over a gentle crest in the ground. Whatever had stolen the corpse had dragged it away.

Larsen jumped to his feet, only to feel Umiak's restraining hand. The man was trembling, and looking at him Larsen saw that his face was pale with fear. 'Don't follow,' said Umiak. 'There may be much danger.'

'From what?' demanded Larsen.

'Bear,' said Umiak. 'Only a grizzly, and a big one at that, could have moved those stones and dragged the body away so easily.'

Larsen was silent for a while. 'You mean he's been eaten?'

'Half eaten, at least. Look!'

Far away down the valley black specks floated in wide lazy circles high in the sky. As they watched, one drifted down, only to rise again and join its fellows. 'Ravens,' observed Umiak. 'They have found what is left. The bear will have eaten its fill and tried to hide the remains, half buried them in the snow or covered them with moss. But it will stay on watch, close to the corpse, and it will attack on sight anything that goes near.'

'So what do we do?' asked Larsen.

'About the body, nothing, except stay right away. The bear will stay with the corpse until there is nothing left. Two days, maybe three. It must be a hungry bear. Usually by now he should have grown fat and sleepy, and be looking for somewhere to den up for his long winter sleep. This one still prowls the hills, so I think the sooner we move out the better.'

'Wouldn't we be safe in the plane?' queried Larsen.

'You can see what the bear did to the grave. How long do you think it would take him to break into the cabin?'

Suddenly Larsen remembered the shadow on the hill and the rattle of stones in the night. His eyes had not been deceiving him, and it occurred to him that he would not have slept so easily had he known what was happening out there under the stars. His fear of the unknown diminished in the face of the greater dread of what fate might befall him here in this lonely valley. 'Right,' he said. 'Let's get out of here.'

'Do you think you could dismantle the control panel of the plane?' asked Umiak.

Larsen shrugged. 'I guess. Why?'

'We could use the wiring behind it. My people, when they hunt the seal or the walrus in their skin kayaks, need many things, rifle, harpoon, lines, knives, and so on. Everything has to be tied to the kayak lest it is washed overboard. I think I can make a sledge from the broken wing of the plane, so we can take with us some fuel and bedding and anything else we may think will come in useful. The going will be rough in places, so everything we take will need to be tied to the sledge or it will be continually falling off. We ought to be ready to move off tomorrow if the weather holds. If deep snow comes, we may be trapped here in the valley.'

Together the two set to work, Larsen stripping electric wiring and control cables from the plane, while Umiak constructed the sledge. They had a small toolkit they found in the plane, a few spanners, pliers, and a couple of screwdrivers, but it was with Larsen's small knife that Umiak did most of the work.

Watching him Larsen could not help being impressed by his dexterity and economy of movement. Seemingly slow and unhurried, his fingers moved so deftly that they appeared to lead a life of their own. Larsen thought again of the arrow-head in his pocket and felt he could begin to understand how these people had survived so successfully for so long.

While he filled freezer bags with petrol, knotting each one tightly before slipping it inside another, Umiak cut two rectangles in the underside of the wing, mitring the corners and folding the edges under so no sharp edges of aluminium remained. Though he measured each one entirely by eye their two holdalls fitted snugly into the recesses. The spaces inside the wing between the cross struts formed a cache for a supply of berries and popcorn.

Most of their spare clothing they donned against the cold. One leg of the dead pilot's trousers replaced that which Larsen had set on fire. Umiak studied the remains of the garment thoughtfully for a while, and then set them to one side. They worked steadily through the day, pausing only for the inevitable meal of popcorn and berries. By now Larsen was so hungry he welcomed even the leaves and other debris mixed in with the fruit.

By late afternoon the sledge was finished. Umiak had used the control cables for hauling lines, and to make all secure he had threaded cable through holes punched along the sides of the wing. In the morning their bedding, rolled in the carpet, could be lashed on top. One holdall was packed with freezer bags containing petrol, each bag representing a day's ration. Umiak did not think the sledge would last very long, but he hoped it would help them at least part of the way. He prayed that it would not snow again too soon, and that the covering that had already fallen would stay firm and wind-packed, at least until they reached lower ground. His final act, before they turned in for the night, was to fashion two pairs of snow goggles, using the tongues and laces of the pilot's boots.

Larsen gazed at the goggles in perplexity. When he put them on he discovered his vision was obscured, except for two tiny slits in the leather. He could barely see a thing. 'I noticed neither you nor the pilot possessed sun glasses,' explained Umiak, 'and mine were broken in the crash. At this time of the year, when the sun is low on the horizon, the light can be very intense, especially when reflected from snow or glare ice. This can cause snow blindness, and believe me, if ever you've suffered from it, it is not an experience you would care to repeat. It can strike in little more than minutes, and though it is rarely permanent it can last for several days. During that time the pain is intense. One way to avoid it is to black your face with soot. Another is to wear these. Perhaps we won't need them, but if we do they will save much torment.'

The last red rays of the sun had faded on the peaks, and in the long slow twilight the temperature began to fall. Despite his earlier fears Larsen felt himself rapidly growing drowsy. The burn on his leg had caused him some discomfort, but the pain was not unbearable, and at least sleep was an antidote to both hunger and cold. He was just drifting into slumber when he heard the howl of the wolves.

He jerked bolt upright, awake in an instant. Beside him Umiak gave a quiet chuckle. 'The old bear will not sleep tonight,' he murmured. 'A wolf pack has come to share in his feast.'

Thereafter Larsen lay wakeful, trying not to let his mind dwell on what might be happening out there. He had never regarded himself as a timid or imaginative man, yet this desolation was getting to him in a way he had never known before. Rather than brood on his fate he tried to analyse his state of mind. After all, he had known more dangerous situations than this. Maybe it was simply that he was growing old and soft.

He thought back to his army days, and the fear he had experienced of the unknown. Then however that fear had been tempered by the company of comrades he knew he could trust. He had been part and parcel of a giant war machine, with access to a radio with which he could call down covering fire, air strike support, speedy evacuation in an emergency. Plus he had weapons of his own.

Here, he was forced to admit, lay the root of the cause of his insecurity. With a repeating rifle by his side, he felt he could face the future with confidence. Yet what in reality had he got to fear? A carrion-eating bear and a distant wolf pack. Unless he were injured or dying he knew he was in no danger from the wolves. The bear presented a threat certainly, but he did not think it would attack unless disturbed. The desire for a weapon, he knew, was not prompted by the fear of any real danger, or even the need to hunt food. It stemmed from a deep yearning, as illogical and yet as real, as the need for a security blanket of a baby.

At least he had companionship, of a sort, in Umiak, who seemed at ease in this wilderness. Umiak had even, he had noticed, lost that irritating giggle, and from the start he had naturally assumed command. He did not seem to be a man who scared easily, and yet he had been visibly afraid of the bear. Perhaps his fears were justified, and if so, the sooner morning came the better.

Another thought bothered him. All the while he had the feeling that as far as Umiak was concerned he was useless freight, dispensable, disposable, a burden to be shed should the occasion warrant it. He had no proof of this, only a nagging doubt he could not be rid of.

Umiak too lay without sleeping. He was fretting about the gun, now pressed uncomfortably against his side. He half wished he had declared its existence from the start, but mistrust and fear had prevented him from doing so. Sooner or later though the white man would come to know of its presence. What would he think, or do? It lay between them, a symbol of power, and there was no way of knowing whether Larsen would respect that power, or try to wrest it from him. It occurred to Umiak simply to throw the gun away, yet even as the thought came to him he dismissed it as untenable. Anyway, it was too late now to produce a reasonable excuse for possessing a concealed weapon. He would just have to deal with the situation if and when it arose. On that philosophical note he fell asleep.

Some of the wolves slept too. The others lay wakeful in the snow, waiting, watchful, the white stars glittering in their eyes. They lay in a wide semicircle, well out of reach of the bear. They were seven in number, a mated pair, two young males, and a trio of half-grown cubs. They had not killed for five days, and the smell of the dead man was strong in their nostrils.

Most of the viscera had been eaten, the liver, kidneys, heart and lungs. Flesh had been torn in great strips from the buttocks and thighs, and part of the face was missing. Much meat still remained, and now the bear moved the carcase, grasping it round the waist in his jaws, and carrying it like a limp rag doll to the shelter of the rocks. Then he lay on guard, one massive curved paw protecting his prize, moaning deep in his throat as he nosed the remains. The wolves moved in to the spot where the corpse had lain to lick the snow and to seek out any stray scraps of skin or flesh. Then they resumed their wait, while the bear stayed wakeful, ready at any moment to kill.

With the coming of the dawn the wolves made their move. Slowly, almost imperceptibly, the pack inched closer, and the drowsing bear woke in terrible rage as the lead wolf ran a few paces towards him. Immediately the wolf backed off, but as the bear subsided his mate ran in from the side.

Instantly the bear lashed out, and had the blow connected it would have crushed her skull like an egg. Wraith-like she swerved aside so that the great claws scythed empty air and spread in the snow. At that moment the male nipped the bear in the hind leg. The bear swung round and charged, and immediately the rest of the pack grabbed at the corpse. At once the bear rushed to retrieve it, seizing it by an arm and biting down so hard that his jaws severed the limb from the body. Bewildered, berserk with fury, the bear dropped the arm to retrieve the greater part of the trunk, so leaving the limb to the wolves.

The bear backed away uphill, dragging the body with him. The wolves followed. The deadly game of tag would continue until there were no spoils left worth fighting for.

6

The morning dawned grey, and a light snow was falling as the two prepared to depart. Umiak muttered and glanced anxiously at the sky, but Larsen was eager to set off. Apart from a nagging hunger he tried to ignore he felt good. His belt, which he had had to let out a couple of notches to accommodate the extra clothing he wore, was now, he noticed, back in its original cinch. The large blister which had formed over the burn in his leg had broken. He made no attempt to cut away the dead skin, but re-dressed the burn with a fresh pad, throwing away the soiled moss and rag.

The makeshift sledge ran smoothly over the frozen wind-packed snow. Earlier Umiak had poured water from the stream over the underside and this had frozen in the cold morning air, forming a protective skin over the aluminium. They had agreed to share the task of pulling it at all times. Larsen had suggested taking turn and turn about, but Umiak had pointed out that an hour's stint pulling the sledge uphill was hardly equal to one on the level. Privately he also realized that such an agreement could lead to bitter disputes over split seconds in time, so he was relieved when Larsen agreed that sharing at all times was fairer.

Though the temperature was well below freezing the dry cold was less chilling than Larsen had feared. What slight breeze there was blew at their backs as they followed the stream along its easterly course. At first the going was easy, but then the stream turned north, and as they gradually lost altitude the ground became more uneven.

Here the valley widened out between the mountain walls, and the river flowed over a flattish plain formed by the deposit of debris and silt over untold centuries. Tussock grass grew in great untidy hummocks, which yielded underfoot, and between them the snow had drifted soft and deep. Each step became an unknown venture, for if one foot found firm support the other was sure to sink into soft yielding snow, so that both men repeatedly fell and floundered. After half an hour of this Umiak suggested they made for higher ground on the flank of the mountain to their right.

To reach it they had to cross about a hundred yards of tussock grass. Without staves to probe the ground ahead every single step had to be considered before they moved. Simply to flounder on was to invite exhaustion and perhaps a wrenched knee, so consequently their progress was painfully slow. Under such conditions, Larsen began to realize, a target of ten miles a day was, to say the least, an optimistic estimate.

High on a ledge above the valley the bear watched the two men depart. The wolves had robbed him of the greater part of his prize and his mood was sullen and angry. He was an old bear, his long shaggy coat unkempt and matted, befouled with carrion and tangled with knots and burrs. His claws were blunt with years of digging for roots and ground squirrels and his teeth were worn from biting earth and bark and bone. His jaws still retained their terrible crushing power though, and his speed when roused could still bring down a running caribou. Yet whenever he moved it was with a pronounced limp, a dipping of the left shoulder that accentuated his rolling gait. It was a legacy of a time when he was overlord of his mountain, supreme master of a hundred square miles of wilderness. He was five summers old, and as yet unaware of the existence of man. On a late autumn morning, with the sun still warm on his back, he was browsing quietly in a berry thicket when he heard the faint metallic click of nailed boot on stone.

The sound had come from downhill, and he reared up on his hind legs the better to observe what manner of beast intruded on his domain. The being was tall, with long thin legs, resembling a caribou coming towards him. Yet even as his mind registered the fact that this was no deer there came a flash and a thunderclap and a violent blow on his arm. There was no pain immediately after. This was to come later, but there was the sight and smell of blood, which always aroused him, and the same anger that even as a tiny cub he had felt after getting the worst of an infant rough-house.

The report of the hunting rifle had caused him to drop out of sight in the undergrowth. Now, as he summoned up all his energy to charge the intruder, he heard the man coming towards him. So he waited and took the hunter from behind.

Only the bear, and the wind that whistled over the tundra knew the exact manner of the man's dying. Those who came searching later found the rifle, with half the stock chewed off. They also found some shreds of clothing, and enough of the skull, with the jaw attached, to identify the hunter from his teeth. Of the bear there was no trace, and the search party did not linger too long on the hill. Better to avoid the region for all time than to walk into the jaws of a killer bear.

Twelve long winters had passed since that time. The wound had healed, and the memory of the pain in his arm had long faded into oblivion. The limp had remained however, a habit acquired in the months it had taken for the pain to pass. So too had the memory of man.

The memory was a legacy of hatred and fear, blended over the years with a recollection of feasting over long days, as the corpse of the hunter rotted in the heat of the autumn sun, while his arm throbbed and burned and gradually stiffened where the bullet had passed through. These memories had been vividly aroused at the grave of the dead pilot.

Now he was past his prime. Had he not been the wolves would never have dared challenge him. As it was, they had taken a considerable risk in the struggle for survival.

As soon as the men were out of sight the bear descended the slope into the valley. He first checked the grave site, but only the scent of carrion lingered to tantalize him further. He prowled round the deserted plane, but there was nothing to attract him there. Moaning softly to himself he padded down to the stream, his great muscles rippling and flowing under his pelt. Flakes of snow drifted down and clung to his fur, lingering without melting except around his eyes and muzzle. He found the soiled moss that Larsen had discarded from his wound and ate it. Then he found the ptarmigan bones scattered among the stones and crunched them into tiny brittle fragments. Still the snow fell, powdering his hide. Like a grey ghost the bear shook his head and set off down the valley, following the trail of the two men.

Out of the tussock the going was easier. The hard-packed snow was firm underfoot, and deep enough to cover all but the larger rocks, but the wind blew stronger on this exposed side of the valley. Frozen particles of moisture stung Larsen's cheeks as he trudged along. To their right the mountains rose like a wall, massive ramparts of rock from which the wind whipped plumes of driven snow. Above the sky was ashen grey.

Somewhere ahead there had to be a break in the mountains. Meantime they travelled north, hour after hour, while ahead of them the valley stretched interminably on, vanishing into a misty veil of driven snow that was like a barrier that receded steadily before them.

Then, abruptly, came a break in the mountains, a narrow defile that sloped gently upwards, seeming to offer a way through. A tiny stream filtered through thickets of low wind-cropped scrub, while on either side the hills rose sheer. Umiak looked at it dubiously. 'Could be a blind canyon,' he muttered.

'Only one way to find out,' observed Larsen. 'At least we'll have the wind on our backs.'

The sky had grown a lighter grey and the snow had ceased to fall, but the wind carried a burden of tiny frozen flakes whipped up from the slopes of the hill as they headed up the gorge. The chasm formed a funnel for the wind, increasing its intensity. It shouted at them now, roaring and whistling up the valley, lashing at them with a thousand needle-pointed stings before howling away in the distance, to be lost among the dark lowering crags that overhung them on either side.

Now massive outcrops of rock barred their way. Several times they had to cross the stream, or skate precariously along the steep slopes of the valley, the sledge skidding along sideways as it hung below them. Twice they had no option but to pick it up and portage it over the rough terrain. At last, exhausted, they collapsed in the lee of a large rock, seeking a moment's respite from the chill of the wind.

'As a boy,' said Larsen, 'I often wondered why the early explorers usually travelled in great circular routes. I think I know why now. It was because nothing on earth would persuade them to turn back and face the obstacles they had already crossed.'

Umiak grunted. 'Unless this wind drops, we cannot turn back. It's forward or nothing for us, and soon we must find a place to spend the night.'

He rose to his feet. Larsen's leg had begun to throb and

burn, and he would have liked to change the dressing, but Umiak was already hitching the towline of the sledge over his shoulder. Larsen took his place at his side.

The way grew steeper, but mercifully the floor of the valley began to widen and flatten out. Ahead of them lay a ridge, flat against the sky, but, as always, when they reached it another appeared on the horizon. Each step became an effort, the cable biting ever harder into Larsen's shoulder, and as the time passed the gnawing ache of hunger began to obsess his thoughts. How long now, he wondered, had it been since he had enjoyed a good meal? Three days, seventy-two hours only, and yet it seemed a lifetime.

Then, abruptly, the way ended. They found themselves in a small hollow, a natural amphitheatre round which the mountains rose on every side. The two men stared in dismay. 'There must be a way out,' exclaimed Larsen.

'There may be,' corrected Umiak. 'But this is not the time to look. We must find shelter, and quickly, for there is much to do.'

To Larsen there seemed to be no place suitable to offer any protection from the cold and wind, but Umiak was already searching among the rocks. He spent a long time, but at last Larsen heard his call. He plodded over, dragging the sledge behind him.

The site Umiak had chosen was no more than a crevice in the rocks, a lidless stone coffin just over six feet long and three feet high. There was barely enough room for the two of them to lie side by side. The only way in was through a narrow slit. It offered some shelter from the wind, but little more. 'The sledge,' asked Umiak 'Will it rest on top?'

It did, though somewhat lopsidedly, and there were gaps all round where it did not touch the rocks. Umiak began at once to stuff these with plugs of snow and moss, but when Larsen tried to help Umiak gestured him away. 'Go and gather bushes to make a bed,' he instructed. 'And pick any berries you can find.'

In the shelter of the rocks bushes grew in plenty, but though the stems were thin they were tough and wiry, scratching Larsen's hands and wrists. He was glad to desist from time to time to harvest berries, both blue and red. Though he returned with a great armful of sprigs Umiak was not satisfied and together the two returned for more. The little shelter was almost packed full before Umiak crawled inside and bounced around chuckling. 'Good, good,' he announced. 'We shall sleep well tonight.'

Larsen was about ready to fall asleep on his feet, but he found energy enough to grumble about supper.

Umiak was cheerful. 'See, we have two sorts of berry tonight, blueberries and cranberries.'

'And popcorn,' groaned Larsen. 'How long can a man survive on just berries?'

'A long time, providing he can find them.'

'But surely,' persisted Larsen, 'soon they'll be all gone, with winter coming on?'

'Not so,' said Umiak. 'I told you, the wilderness is a good place. If the fall season was long and mild, the berries would become overripe and rotten, fermenting in the sun. Here the cold preserves them, and so plenty of berries last all winter. They stay fresh, and in the spring they are juicier and fresher than ever. My people know this, and look for them then. Trouble is that the bears know this too, and it is the first food they look for when they wake from their winter sleep. So berry picking can be dangerous in the spring, but berries are good for bears and men.'

'They don't do much to satisfy a man's hunger though,' complained Larsen. 'We must have eaten pounds, but I still feel empty.'

'They eat best mixed with meat and fat,' admitted Umiak. 'I'll set some snares before we turn in. Maybe we'll get lucky.'

Despite his weariness and Umiak's confident predictions, Larsen slept badly. He was cold, his leg hurt, and the warmth of their bodies awakened myriads of tiny biting flies that had lain concealed and dormant in their bush bedding. Umiak slept undisturbed, but Larsen merely dozed fitfully, and when he did it was to dream of food, steaks sizzling on a barbecue, bacon frying in a pan, the crisp golden fat crinkling at the edges, fried eggs swimming in a sea of aromatic fat.

Not far away the bear too dozed the night away. He also was hungry and from time to time he raised his muzzle, his dark nose questing the air. There was a smell of man, which hitherto he had hated and feared. Yet there was too a faint whiff of the sickly sweet scent of putrefaction and decay, the scent that had led him to the cairn on the hill. There too had been the odour of man, and there had been nothing there to fear.

Most of his life the bear had spent feeding on vegetation, young grasses in the spring, roots of stunted poplar and bark of willows when the sap was running and they were full of starch, berries when the crop was thickest. Yet almost every day he got some meat, the young of a ground-nesting bird, a squirrel, voles, lemmings, a snow-shoe hare. From time to time he would come upon dead caribou calves, or sick or injured adults. Such a prize was a feast, and the higher and riper the carcase the better he liked it. Now his nose told him that an injured man lay not far away, and though he feared to approach too close as yet, his old brain told him that the time would come when he would feast on flesh again. So he hungered and slept, snug in his thick pelt, while the frosting of snow that had fallen earlier clung unmelted to the long outer guard hairs.

7

There was a way out, or so it seemed. It was little more than a cleft in the mountain wall, a crack in the rim of the basin in which they had spent the night. It rose steeply, a tortured staircase of terraced rocks and ledges, elbowing round out of sight to be lost in the cloud vapours that capped the barren peaks.

The two men looked at it dubiously. For all they knew it might end at an unscalable wall of rock or slippery slope of scree. Nor was there any way they could drag the sledge up there. It would have to be portaged every inch of the way. They debated whether to make a preliminary reconnaissance, but in the end set off carrying the sledge between them.

Almost at once Larsen slipped on the ice-covered rocks and fell, bruising his shoulder and cursing with anger and pain. Umiak dug out the remains of the dead pilot's trousers and cut strips of cloth from them, making bindings for their boots so as to give them a better grip on the steep and slippery ground. Even so the going was rough. They could not climb together. Larsen, in the lead, would gain a foot or so, then take the load of the sledge while Umiak followed. Then it was Umiak's turn to bear the weight, perched precariously on rock that was ice-bound and rotten, while Larsen scrabbled for a fresh foothold, sending a shower of small stones and occasionally larger rocks cascading down. The sledge banged and rattled against the rocks in spite of all their care, but Umiak's improvised lashings held, and nothing was lost.

At length Umiak cried out for a rest. 'Too hot,' he complained.

'Makes a change,' grunted Larsen, impatient for their ordeal to end.

'Not good,' said Umiak. 'Sweat now, we freeze later. The wind will be cold at the top.' So they rested, while Larsen fumed at the delay. His leg felt easier for the night's rest. He had changed the dressing, clipping away the dead skin from over the blistered area. The wound was fiery and inflamed, and discharging freely, but the lymph was clear, with no sign of suppuration. He would have preferred to have left the wound open to the air to dry, but he feared the effects of the cold. Besides, the moss pad was a comfort. He renewed it, throwing away the soiled moss, but retaining the bandages in the hope that he would be able to wash them and use them again.

After a short break they moved on. They were in cloud now, and above them the wind moaned as it prowled restlessly between the peaks. The way grew easier, and an hour later they emerged on to a flat plateau of bare basaltic rock. Here the wind took them and savaged them, tearing at their clothing and threatening to throw them off their feet.

Flat on their faces they crawled the last few yards over the summit. At first they could see nothing. Icy mist swirled and eddied around them, the wind stung their eyes and snatched their breath away. Then, abruptly, the skies cleared, the veils were ripped away, and they found themselves looking down on the thin black thread of a river far below them, winding its way over a tapestry of snow, rose-pink and white, stippled with fawn and gold. In front of them and to their left the mountain fell sheer, black precipitous rock dusted with wind-driven snow. To the south the shoulder of the hill sloped away in a gentle curve. It seemed the only way down.

After the arduous climb of the morning the descent was relatively easy and swift, but now ahead lay the broad snow-covered valley, stretching endlessly away to the north. To the east lay more mountains to cross, more valleys to traverse, a limitless, lifeless expanse of snow and ice and barren rock. Larsen thrust all thoughts of the future from him and plodded on, walking because exertion was preferable to inaction. At least the wind had moderated somewhat, and the cloud was thin and high, with now and then a glimpse of pale sun. Once Umiak shouted and pointed at something ahead of them. At first Larsen could see nothing, only the black rocks and scattered drifts of snow on the mountain-side. Then a tiny speck of white detached itself from a larger drift and moved slowly over the landscape. Others followed, and as they leaped into focus Larsen saw that they were wild sheep, grazing on the distant hillside. He shrugged and walked on. They were too far away to be of interest, though Umiak seemed inordinately excited. Without a rifle to bring one down, the sheep were as inaccessible as if they were on the moon.

The sight of them though reminded Larsen of his hunger. There had been no ptarmigan in the snares that morning, and even the popcorn was running low. Anyway his system craved meat, hot meat, red and running with fat. At the thought saliva filled his mouth and he felt his stomach contract in a sudden gripping knot that made him catch his breath. It was the first and mildest of the hunger pains that were to seize him in the days to come. Thereafter they were to grow more frequent, and more severe.

The river was shallow and swift flowing, but nowhere was it narrow enough to jump. Rather than face the discomfort of wading across through the icy water they veered upstream, hoping to find a place where they could cross dry-shod. As they rounded a bend a rock lying on a gravel bar suddenly woke to life and flapped heavily away. While Larsen watched the bald eagle climb up into the sky Umiak dropped the towline of the sledge and went running down to the water's edge.

A fish lay there, or rather the remains of one, for the eagle had eaten about a third. Several pounds of flaccid spongy pink flesh still clung to the carcase, that of a spawned-out salmon, plucked from the river in its dying moments by the bird. The two men looked at it, trembling with anticipation. Larsen ran back to the sledge and got the fuel and stove. Umiak prepared a pit in the sand-bar and lined it with a plastic bag. Soon chunks of flesh were curding in the fragrant steam.

The fish was well past its prime, for its muscles had begun to degenerate even before it had spawned. Still, the meat was hot and filling and they stayed until they had finished the lot. Rather Umiak did, for after a while Larsen began to feel uncomfortably full. By then the stew had cooled in the Arctic air to the point where it was no more than unpleasantly tepid. Thereafter the sight of Umiak still eating provoked a wave of nausea, so that Larsen began to fear he would lose what nourishment he had already got. It occurred to him to suggest they ought to save some meat for later, but the idea of eating cold fish repelled him, and Umiak seemed to have no such intention.

He moved away from the sight and smell of the fish, aware that in addition to his physical nausea he was experiencing a sense of shame and self-disgust at being reduced to the plight of a carrion eater, a scavenger upon a scavenger. Was this the natural role of mankind in the wild, he wondered, on a par with the jackal, the hyaena, and the turkey buzzard? He remembered reading how, if the early fur traders lingered too long in the wild, and were caught by the winter so that they were unable to paddle their canoes down the frozen waterways, they were forced to 'eat crow'. Since then the expression had come to mean any admission of guilt or error. At least his predicament was not brought about by any sin of omission, and anyway, there was no shame in a man living on his wits. Thus comforted, and presently lulled by the sound of the stream flowing by at his feet he fell asleep.

The smell of man was strong again, and there was more of the moss, the salty savour of which he had relished the previous morning. Cautiously the bear approached the niche in the rocks where the two men had spent the night. The fear of man still lingered, though it was waning with increased familiarity. A sudden noise or movement now might have sent the bear bolting away up the hill with all the considerable speed a grizzly can muster, but nothing like this occurred.

With surprising ease the bear poured his huge bulk into the niche, passing through the gap in the rocks in one fluid rippling movement. Inside, his questing snout explored every corner in a series of loud snorts. Then, satisfied that nothing edible lay hidden away, he shook up the bedding, curled himself in a ball and fell asleep.

Hunger woke him later in the day. Again the man scent was strong in the mountain defile, and the bear quickened his pace. He lost the trail for a while on the summit but soon found it again on the downward sloping ridge. He tracked the men upstream, and lingered a moment over the fish head and bones. Then he moved on to where a partial bridge of water-worn stone restricted the width of the stream and enabled him to cross the river without getting wet, as it had done earlier for Larsen and Umiak. On the far bank a ground squirrel eluded him until it was almost dark, though he made earth and stones fly in all directions in his efforts to dig it out. At length, cornered, the squirrel died suddenly and violently, though in the end it was no more than a savoury morsel for the bear.

Still he loitered, masticating roots and grass torn up by his exertions, while a thin snow began to fall and to cover the men's tracks. It did not matter to the bear, whose sense of smell could detect a squirrel under three feet of snow or the birth of a caribou calf from over a mile down wind. The dead pilot's trousers bore the faint but unmistakable taint of death and by making boot bindings out of them Umiak had laid a trail the bear could follow even if it was a week old. Now, unless distracted or diverted from his intent, wherever the men went the bear would follow, lured on by the lingering taint of decay, which more and more was becoming associated in his mind with the scent of man.

The snow fell thicker, adding to the sprinkling already frozen to the bear's long pelt. The heat of his body had melted some of the snow, turning it to moisture that had trickled down the guard hairs of his chest and flanks. Here, in contact with the icy air, it had frozen again to form long thin icicles, a curtain of ice that jingled faintly but musically with every movement he made. If the bear was aware of this he gave no sign, made no attempt to groom himself. As the light faded he merged into the gloom, a ghost bear at one with the snow-covered landscape and the pitiless Arctic night.

A few miles to the south-east Umiak and Larsen were preparing to pass what promised to be a long and uncomfortable night. The best they had been able to find in the way of shelter was an overhang of rock halfway up the hillside in a long narrow pass through the mountains. They had gone supperless, and now, at Umiak's suggestion, they sat back to back, a pile of bedding insulating them from the cold, the carpet wrapped around them.

Sleep eluded them. The snowstorm passed, the stars

burned white in an indigo sky, then paled as at first faintly and then with growing intensity flickering ribbons of green and white light flashed across the sky, illuminating the mountains beyond and bathing them in a soft ethereal glow. Despite his misery Larsen felt a thrill of exhilaration at the spectacle. 'Beats fourth of July fireworks,' he murmured.

'Ghost dancers,' said Umiak. 'Northern lights. My people once believed they were the spirits of the dead. Now we are told they are caused by an electro-magnetic storm high above the earth, but that doesn't lessen their beauty, or their mystery.'

He stirred uneasily. 'This pass we are following. It is leading us too far to the south. We must try and head north again, or we'll be lost in the mountains.'

'How do you know?' queried Larsen.

'At this time of night the bands of light always flow at right angles to the poles of the earth.'

Larsen digested this in silence. It did not seem to strike Umiak as at all incongruous that the ghosts of his ancestors should act as navigational aids to the living. Larsen's euphoria began to wane as the cold bit deeper. If only they were properly outfitted, warm and well fed, how different their situation would be. He could almost conceive of himself enjoying it. Inevitably his thoughts returned to the unknown terrain that lay ahead, and the equally incalculable distance they would have to travel before they reached civilization. 'If only we had a snow machine,' he muttered, more to himself than his companion.

'Those things,' scoffed Umiak. 'They'd be useless in these hills. Okay on level ground, I guess, but even then they spend more time stripped down on the work bench than on the trail. Anyway, they're noisy, dangerous and cold. Dog teams are better. At least if a dog is injured or killed you can always eat it or feed it to the others. You can't eat a snowmobile.'

Nettled by this summary dismissal of western technology, Larsen felt somehow bound to defend it. 'If snow machines are such a lousy idea, how come your people buy so many of them?'

'How come your people abandoned the horse for the automobile? When they work, snow machines go faster, travel further than dogs. For going to the store, meeting the mail plane, hauling garbage to the dump, they're more convenient. Dogs are trouble. They fight, run away, steal your food. They take a lot of handling on the trail. They have to be fed, whether you are working or not. When you don't need a snow machine you park it and forget it.

'In the early days we were encouraged to buy snow machines, because then we had to go to work to earn dollars, instead of staying home fishing and hunting for food for our dogs. It takes a lot of meat to support a dog team, and it was hoped that the snow machine would help conserve fish and caribou stocks. Maybe it did for a while, but a lot of people are going back to dogs now.'

'How far would a dog team carry us in a day?' asked Larsen.

'Depends. Fifty, a hundred miles a day, according to the trail, the weather, how good a team you got, and how hard you push them.'

Larsen sighed. Two days, and they could be out of this. So far they'd travelled about twenty miles, mostly in the wrong direction. He wondered how much longer they could endure, how long they could survive the cold and the growing starvation. He was acutely aware that at any time some accident could befall them, some freak of weather trap them and hold them prisoner until they died. He realized then that he had given up all hope of an early rescue.

As if in response to his unspoken thoughts Umiak said softly, 'Only the now is real. The future does not exist, any more than the past.'

Umiak's words had a strangely oriental ring, and Larsen was struck again by the thought that he was at the meeting place of East and West, where the spirits of the departed signposted the way on a journey that was without end.

The display of lights faded. In response the stars brightened, and the mountain peaks merged with the sky. In the silence of the night a sudden sound startled the two men into instant alertness. It came again, the faint but harsh clatter of a stone. Larsen felt Umiak stiffen, heard the pounding of his own heart as he strained his ears in the darkness.

It came again, nearer this time. Something was moving on the hill above them. Then, with the scrape of stone came a soft panting sound, deep and ominous. Beside him Umiak began to tremble and in spite of the cold Larsen felt his hands grow moist with perspiration. 'What is it?' he whispered.

'Bear, I think.' Umiak swallowed and licked his lips. 'Listen, when I tell you, not before, yell as loud and as long as you can.'

Larsen waited. Long seconds passed, each an eternity in a silence more profound, more terrifying than any he had experienced in the prelude to a Vietcong attack. He felt his stomach contract with fear and it took all his willpower to sit still, determined not to tremble, locking his muscles rigid in an effort to control them.

There was no further warning. Simultaneously both men saw the bear. It had circled round and was approaching them from below, its massive bulk suddenly rearing up from the snow. 'Now,' whispered Umiak, and the two yelled at the top of their voices.

One moment the bear was there, and the next it had vanished without a sound, and there was no indication of how far it had gone, or for how long. As the minutes passed and the bear did not return Larsen noticed that Umiak had ceased trembling and now seemed quite composed. He found this strangely reassuring, for he had been baffled and somewhat shaken by the other man's obvious terror, both now and on previous occasions. It seemed at once disproportionate and out of character in a man who did not appear to scare easily. Suddenly Larsen realized that Umiak would know that he had not been able to conceal his fear. Maybe he was brooding on the fact right now, and supposing that the white man considered him a coward.

Was he, though? Was his fear inbred, or was it born of experience? Larsen felt he had to know, or at least pass some comment to show that he understood. 'If you don't mind me saying so,' he began, 'you seemed pretty scared for a while back there. Serious, huh?'

Umiak's voice was low, but it was steady, without a trace of hysteria or fear. 'I have seen what a bear can do to a man. I lost my brother that way, when I was just a kid. They will play with you, feast on you while you are still alive. Seems they've never learned to kill clean, or don't want to. Sometimes, if you scream, they will bite you, in the leg or the groin, just to make you scream louder...'

'Yes, well I think I'd rather not know,' said Larsen hurriedly. 'I guess it took guts for you to sit there, knowing what you do.'

'There was nowhere to go,' said Umiak simply.

'Do you think he will return?' asked Larsen.

Umiak considered a moment. 'Not tonight,' he said finally. 'He's had a bad scare. I think he was expecting to find us dead.'

'Like our pilot,' said Larsen. 'So he's the same bear,' he added, more to himself than Umiak.

'The same,' replied Umiak. 'A bear with a taste for human flesh.'

8

Despite the fear, despite the cold and hunger and the discomfort of sitting upright with nowhere to rest his head, Larsen slept. He woke to the rumble of thunder, and opened his eyes on a world of shifting light, as black clouds swirled and eddied around the bleak and desolate landscape, and stray snowflakes drifted on the wind that whistled and roared up the pass.

To move on seemed folly, yet neither man felt inclined to linger a moment longer than necessary in what could soon become a rocky tomb among the mountains. Their preparations were brief. They ate the last of the popcorn and the few remaining berries, melted some snow for a hot drink, and after luxuriating until the last moment in the warmth of the flames they set off into the gloom. The thunder still muttered and growled, and vivid lightning flashes lit the surrounding peaks and crags which towered high above them, so that they seemed to lean towards them as if threatening to come crashing down and annihilate them.

They plodded on in silence. Larsen felt weak and light-headed. His leg ached and throbbed, every step sending a spasm of pain shooting up into his knee and thigh, and all the while the pressure of the bandage seemed to be increasing. He had not changed the dressing that morning, for there had been no moss among the litter of stones where they had passed the previous night. As they climbed upward the snow grew deeper, sticky and soft, dragging at their feet and adding to the burden of the sledge.

Vainly they searched for a way out to the north. One route presented itself, a narrow tortuous defile which seemed to lead over a saddle between two peaks. They hesitated for a while and then passed on, hoping to find an easier route. An hour later they reached the foot of the glacier.

It stretched before them for over a mile before vanishing into the clouds, an awesome tangle of rock and grey, fissured ice, ridged with pressure waves and split by tortured crevasses. Without ice-axes and ropes there was no way they could get themselves or the sledge across. There was nothing for it but to turn back, seek the defile they had passed on the way up, and hope it afforded a way out.

Twice they despaired of ever making it to the top. Time after time they had to turn the sledge on its side to angle it around protruding boulders that barred their way, Umiak leading and Larsen bringing up the rear, favouring his injured leg and perspiring freely in spite of the cold. Each fresh foothold brought a moment's anxiety, lest he should slip and fall, breaking a leg or twisting his knee, and always in the back of his mind was the haunting fear of the bear, lingering somewhere near, growing ever bolder as increasing hunger drove it on.

He was only dimly aware they had reached the summit. He lay face down on the frozen ground, the cold air rasping his lungs, his breathing harsh and loud as his clamouring heart strove to supply his system with the oxygen it craved. At length he recovered sufficiently to sit up, only to find that Umiak had disappeared. Sudden panic seized him and he was about to call out, when he heard a rattle of stones and the other man reappeared. He looked thoughtful and grave.

'There's a break in the mountain ahead,' he announced, 'a crevasse barring our way. It looks narrow enough to jump, but...'

'But what?' queried Larsen.

'There's only one way to find out, and if I'm wrong, it's a long way to the bottom.'

Larsen could only stand and wonder at the violent primeval forces that had split the solid rock. Only an earthquake of some magnitude could have shaken the mountain to that degree. The path ended in a knife-edged drop, the brink of a chasm which widened on either side of them. The opposite lip looked almost close enough to touch, but its edge was raised perhaps a foot higher than their side. Beneath, the sheer rock face sloped away under their feet so that they were unable to see the depths to which it plunged, a fact which did nothing to allay Larsen's fears. As he studied the gap, it seemed to grow wider.

They tried to bridge it with the sledge, but it was inches short, and they almost lost all their possessions in the black void below. Then without warning Umiak took hold of the towline and jumped.

He cleared the gap with inches to spare, landing nimbly on the far side. Then he turned and waited. Larsen pushed the sledge out over the crevasse towards him, and as it hung on the point of balance Umiak heaved on the towline, Larsen gave a final push in unison, and their goods were safely across. Larsen poised himself to leap, then checked, and it was this hesitation that proved his undoing.

If he took off on his bad leg, he was not sure he could clear the gap. If he used his good leg, he would jar the injured one on landing. So he wavered, and all the time the gap seemed to him to grow wider. He was about to ask Umiak to throw him one end of the towline when a look of horror crossed the man's face. 'Jump, man, quick,' he yelled. 'The bear!'

Larsen jumped, clearing the gap with ease, and landing neatly beside Umiak on the level surface of the rock. He turned to look back, expecting to see the bear, but there was nothing, only the bare rock and the clouds. To his astonishment Umiak began to laugh.

He saw then that he had been tricked, that Umiak had thought he had lost his nerve, and been afraid to jump. So he had gambled on the fact that Larsen's fear of the bear would prove greater than his fear of falling, and it had worked.

He was a man slow to anger, not given to violent aggressive ways. He had seriously doubted, when he had joined the army, whether he could actually kill a man, even an enemy, in personal combat. He was to learn that he could. His platoon was hunting down a few stray guerrillas, driven from hiding in a jungle village, when his best friend was shot by a stray bullet.

The wound was a minor one, a near miss, the bullet creasing the man's cheek, slitting the strap of his steel helmet and laying the flesh open to the bone. As the man's headgear slid sideways Larsen saw the sliver of skin fly away from his friend's face, watched the white bone flower with crimson, and as the man pitched over it seemed he was wearing an insane grin that split his features from mouth to ear.

At that instant the stupidity and senselessness of it all struck Larsen as the ultimate in obscenitys and, leaping forward he fired into the bush from which the shot came. There was a sharp scream and the Vietcong emerged, a mere boy, his weaponless hands held out in surrender, his face twisted in a smile of mingled fear and supplication. Larsen had kept firing, until his magazine was empty and the head and shoulders of the corpse a pulp of red meat. He had then flung aside the gun in self-disgust.

Now Umiak had evoked that same sense of revulsion. Hatred of the man's devious ways, his own humiliation and weakness, plus a bitter resentment at the way Umiak had seemed to dominate their partnership ever since the time of the plane crash, boiled up inside him in an explosion of insane rage. For Umiak was laughing, and this was the ultimate insult. A low moan of anger began deep in his throat. It grew to a bellow of animal savagery, and he sprang.

Umiak saw the attack coming, but he was powerless to check the first onslaught. The two men fell heavily, Larsen on top, his hands around Umiak's throat and his thumbs digging deep into the carotid arteries. Umiak brought his arms up inside Larsen's, his fists clenched, driving a double hammer blow to Larsen's chin. As the man's head whiplashed back Umiak's arms swept out and down, breaking the stranglehold and flinging him clear.

As he struggled to his feet Larsen came again, head down, half crazed with frustration and rage. Umiak brought his knee up and heard the wind go out of Larsen as he connected with the man's midriff, but then they were rolling on the ground again, Larsen's arms were locked around his waist, and they were perilously close to the brink of the abyss.

Though slender for his height, Umiak was as tough as the rawhide cords on which he had been hauling all his life, and wrestling was a national sport among his people. Grimly he twisted in Larsen's grip, forced himself to his knees, and then to his feet. With a quick heave he threw Larsen over one hip, and slammed him to the ground. He felt the man weaken, and then relax his grip entirely. As Larsen sat up he stepped back, and as he did so the revolver slipped from his belt and clattered down on the rock between them.

Larsen, sobbing from weakness and despair, stared at it dully. It lay squat and black and ugly, its muzzle pointing towards him like an unblinking eye. A moment ago he might have grabbed it and used it, but now he made no move towards it, merely watching as Umiak picked it up and stowed it back in his waistband.

He began instead to roll up his trouser leg and unwrap the bandage that protected his wound. It was a gesture of submission, an acknowledgement of defeat as old as mankind. Umiak watched impassively as Larsen peeled off the last remaining shreds of cloth and exposed the weeping ulcerated sore. Larsen gathered a hardful of snow and held it to the site, wincing at first and then relaxing as the cold anaesthetized the pain. He closed his eyes with relief, and when he opened them again Umiak was standing beside him, holding fresh bandages, and also a plastic bag filled with moss he must have gathered previously and stowed away in the sledge.

It was a peace offering, and Larsen recognized it as such, feeling greatly reassured, for it occurred to him that a man who had had the foresight and thought to pack the moss was hardly likely to blow his brains out. With the realization came a renewed sense of inadequacy, for he himself should have made such provision.

The leg was a mess. His calf was inflamed from knee to ankle, and where the blister had broken there was now a circle of weeping flesh, from the centre of which yellow pus oozed under pressure. He could do no more than bind it up again, and hope it would stand up to the strain of walking.

Umiak regarded him dubiously. He wondered if there would be a repetition of the morning's events, and decided not, unless, that was, the man's mind went completely. The possibility was not as remote as it seemed. Larsen was close to breaking point, and would have to be nursed along. Nor could he tell how long Larsen could keep going physically.

He sighed, staring about him. Dark clouds still wreathed the peaks, which seemed to close in jagged disarray around them. Until the skies cleared, he had no way of knowing what direction in which to head. Meantime, it would do them no harm to rest.

'You a good shot?' asked Larsen suddenly.

Umiak shrugged. 'I can take the eye out of a seal at two hundred feet.' It was a statement of fact rather than a boast. 'But that's in a good light, with a rifle. Revolvers are for close work.'

'Like on the bear,' suggested Larsen.

Umiak shrugged. 'I hope it never comes to that. There's no way this would stop a bear before he'd killed you. It would only serve to infuriate him more. Better to turn it on yourself.'

Larsen digested this in silence. 'Well,' he said at length, 'if you come across anything worth shooting, make sure you don't miss. Me, I was never any good with sidearms.'

It was, thought Umiak, a sign of surrender, at least an acknowledgement that he held the gun. He hoped, if the time came, he would not fail the other man's trust. Meanwhile, he felt, the whole matter had been resolved quite satisfactorily.

Gradually he began to grow drowsy. Beside him Larsen sat propped against a rock, his eyes closed, his chin resting on his chest. They both needed rest after their wakeful night, and until the weather cleared they had no inkling of which direction they should take. Rising to his feet he began to unpack the bedding from the sledge.

Larsen came to with a jerk, and then, rising stiffly, limped over to help. 'I thought travellers who fell asleep in the cold never woke up,' he remarked.

Umiak laughed. 'My people have been falling asleep all over the place for ten thousand years. Most of them woke up eventually. We'll sleep until the weather clears.'

'What about the bear?' asked Larsen.

Umiak glanced back the way they had come. 'Don't worry. He won't cross that gap. Bears can't jump.'

Hunger pains woke Larsen later in the day. The skies

cleared, but the Arctic wind still moaned and sighed among the rocks. Somewhere behind the mountains the sun still shone, and the snowfields blushed rose-pink in the reflected light. Leaving Umiak to sleep Larsen crawled from under the carpet and set off uphill, following a gentle rise that led to a nearby summit, and from which he hoped he could get a view of the terrain that lay beyond.

He felt fresher, and the pain in his leg had subsided to a dull ache, but rather ruefully he noted that he had sustained several bruises in his brawl with Umiak. Either the guy was incredibly tough, or he was getting soft. He ought to have spent more time during the past years working out in the gym, and less time belting back scotch in the bar. Still, he felt strangely purged, of both bitterness and anger, and, in fairness, Umiak, didn't appear to be the sort to bear a grudge.

He reached the peak he was aiming for, and the view burst upon him with a shock that was like a jolt to the heart. He stood on a high crag, and the rock face below him fell away sheer for a thousand feet. As far as the eye could see there were mountains fading into the misty distance. Between lay a chain of small lakes, glittering in the cold northern light, and interlinked by the winding silver ribbons of streams. Vast snow-fields lay against the slopes of the hills, swept there by the relentless driving wind. Elsewhere the land was bare, brown and sere, except in the hollows around the lakes, where carpets of green and gold revealed patches of tundra.

The beauty and the grandeur of the scene made him forget his present plight, and for a brief moment the professional in him took over, desperately wondering how he could sell such a magnificent panorama to his clients. He could see now why the region was known as the Gates of the Arctic. Then despair descended as he realized how far he still had to travel. Seen from this altitude, the wilderness seemed greater, more isolated, more overwhelming and intimidating than he had so far imagined, and for the first time he began seriously to wonder if it was worth even making the effort to cross such a vast distance. It would be so much easier just to lie down, make himself as comfortable as possible and await the gentle caress of death. At that precise moment he heard the thin whip-crack of a pistol shot and, turning, he began to run back the way he had come.

9

'An owl!' exclaimed Larsen. 'You wasted a bullet on a lousy owl?'

'Not a lousy owl, a snowy owl,' laughed Umiak. 'When I woke she was sitting on that rock just there. I couldn't miss. Now we have plenty of meat, and good eating too.' He held the great bird up by the talons so that the wings hung down half spread. Most of the head had been blown away, and the snow-white plumage, heavily barred with brown, was spattered with tiny droplets of crimson. There was, Larsen had to admit, plenty of meat. Even without the head the carcase was almost two feet in length, and must have weighed almost seven pounds.

Expertly Umiak began to strip the feathers from the still palpitating corpse. 'Women's work,' he remarked cheerfully. 'But we must shift for ourselves.'

They ate slowly, savouring every morsel, and Larsen was agreeably surprised to find that Umiak had told him no lie, and that the flesh was tender and appetizing. Replete at last, he sat back with a sigh, although half the owl remained uneaten, and though Umiak looked wistfully at the chunks of meat still floating among the broth he too refrained from helping himself further. The soupy stew slowly congealed in the plastic bag, and by and by Umiak picked out the stones they had used in cooking it, and after licking each one clean threw them away. The remains of the stew they carefully sealed and stowed away in the sledge.

They made little further progress that day. To lose height they had to follow the long sloping shoulder of a ridge and finally make a hair-raising descent over a patch of steep scree. By evening they had reached the first of the lakes, where they had hopes of finding fish, but to their disappointment the waters were encased in a layer of ice, too thin to bear their weight. They turned instead to the stream, but the shallow waters seemed devoid of life. So they went supperless to bed, but at least their worst hunger had been allayed, and they had the remainder of the owl to look forward to.

For the next two days they journeyed on through the mountains, picking a tortuous route among a maze of narrow passes and defiles, wending their way past frozen lakes and glaciers, following the course of any stream that led roughly east. Twice they had to labour over rocky saddles, when mountains barred their path. The weather held fine, and though the sun hung low on the horizon its rays sent a thin warmth through their bones, although to step into the shade was like entering a refrigerated room.

Nights brought relief from the wearisome toil of the day, but misery of a different kind. Despite all their endeavours to keep warm the cold seemed to permeate their very bones. Long hours passed in wakefulness, and increasing cold and hunger pains robbed them of sleep well before dawn. Hunger and lack of sleep combined to weaken them still further: their legs felt leaden and useless, so that each step required a conscious effort of will.

Dusk of the second day found them plodding wearily upwards through a narrow gorge, following a stream to its source, with the certain knowledge that they would have yet another mountain to cross. The sun had sunk out of sight, the temperature was falling, and they had almost despaired of finding shelter for the night when Larsen noticed the cave.

The entrance was low and rounded, as though enlarged by some animal in the past, but the snow that had drifted into the entrance was devoid of tracks. Larsen peered cautiously into the darkness. 'What do you think?' he whispered.

Umiak bit his thumb. 'I dunno. Could be occupied. Bear or wildcat perhaps. Better make sure. Even a wolverine could be dangerous if cornered.' He picked up a rock and, motioning Larsen to one side, he lobbed it as far as he could into the cave. It landed with a soft thud.

'Sand,' suggested Larsen.

'Or fur,' said Umiak. He tried another stone, with the same result. Still he hesitated, and Larsen began to lose patience. Somehow he was sure the cave was uninhabited, and suddenly he saw a chance to overcome his earlier humiliation by Umiak. If the man was scared to take a look, he wasn't.

Before Umiak could stop him he had dropped on all fours and crawled through the entrance. Immediately the cave widened out, so he could no longer touch the walls, and he pulled the cigarette lighter from his pocket, ready to use it if need be. The floor was of soft dry sand, and he moved to his right until he came in contact with the wall, intending to follow it round, or retrace his steps if the cave proved to be of any great size.

There was no taint of animal odour. Instead the air smelled musty and strangely familiar, a scent associated with childhood, with schooldays. Suddenly, in the darkness, recognition came to him, the place smelled like a museum. He moved on. The wall curved steadily towards the left. Evidently the cave was not very large, about ten feet in diameter he guessed.

Then he recoiled in sudden terror, and he was barely

able to stifle a sudden yelp of fear. His hand had touched fur. He knelt, frozen, hardly daring to breathe, waiting and listening for any sign of life. There was nothing, and very gingerly he stretched out his hand again. It was certainly skin or hide of some sort, but whatever it had been was now long dead, cold and lifeless to the touch. Larsen decided it was time to take a look. He flicked the lighter, and the flame sprang up, clear and bright.

The body of a man, clad in furs, lay upon a pile of caribou skins. His face was black and wrinkled and shiny as leather, his eyeless sockets staring sightlessly up at the ceiling. For a long moment Larsen stared at the mummified corpse, wondering how many years, centuries perhaps, had passed since he had been laid to rest there. Then, mindful of the need to conserve fuel, he snapped off the lighter and crawled back to report his find to Umiak.

Together they lifted the topmost skin and the corpse off the pile and laid it gently against one wall of the cave. It was feather light, but the cold dry air of the cave had mummified the remains in an almost perfect state of preservation. It was as they were spreading the rest of the skins to make a couch for the night that Umiak kicked something with an unmistakable metallic clang.

It was a quart-sized canteen of the sort supplied by the thousand in the era of the fur trade. Umiak bore it outside in triumph and filled it with snow while Larsen prepared the stove. In the flickering light of the petrol flames they were able to see further into the gloom. There was a skin bag containing a residue of black powder which Umiak guessed had once been dried meat and berries. There was a stone lamp and a poke that still contained oil, now thick and black and tarry. There was a flint and steel and tinder and a pair of fur-lined sealskin boots, iron hard with age. Best of all, there was a homemade knife with a handle made from caribou antler.

As they settled for the night Larsen voiced the

question that had been puzzling him ever since he had found the body. How had it got there, and why?

'He was abandoned,' said Umiak shortly.

'How can you tell?' queried Larsen.

'It all adds up,' said Umiak. 'He wouldn't be up here on his own, with a pile of caribou skins and no weapons. He must have been with a hunting party, and he was left, with food and fire and a couch to lie on.'

'Do you suppose he was hurt?' asked Larsen. 'Too badly injured to walk?'

'No,' said Umiak slowly. 'They would have carried him. My guess is that they were afraid, and that suggests he had some sort of infectious disease, smallpox or measles, or diphtheria. So they abandoned him to recover or die, while they fled in fear.'

'Seems exceptionally callous somehow,' said Larsen with a shiver.

'It was their only chance of survival,' answered Umiak. 'Whole villages died in epidemics of that kind. My people had no resistance to white man's disease, and even a cold could kill them.'

Larsen felt his flesh crawl at the thought of microbes from the distant past, perfectly preserved in the confines of this cave, waiting to claim yet another victim. Then he relaxed. 'I've had measles,' he remarked, 'and I've been vaccinated and immunized against most other infectious diseases.'

'So have I,' said Umiak. 'Progress is a marvellous thing.'

It occurred to Larsen that there was an ironic ring to Umiak's voice, but he chose not to pursue it. He fell asleep easier than usual, but his dreams were haunted by brown-skinned men, their faces purulent with running sores.

He woke to find Umiak busy. He had taken the sealskin boots and was trying to restore their suppleness by rubbing in the thick tarry residue of oil which was left in the sealskin poke. The smell was revolting, but Umiak seemed unconcerned. 'There was a time,' he remarked casually, 'when a woman's first duty on waking was to take her husband's frozen boots and chew on them until they were warm and supple. I guess high school has changed all that. I can't see today's young brides taking on such duties. There's no need now anyway, what with kerosene stoves and central heating and boots made of rubber.'

He bent back to his work. Larsen watched him in the dim light that now filtered through into the cave, wondering whether he dare voice the question in his mind. 'You married, Umiak?'

There was a pause. 'Was once,' said Umiak.

Another silence followed, so long that Larsen began to think that Umiak was not prepared to volunteer any further information. Then Umiak spoke again. 'I was away at the time. There was an outbreak of polio. She and the two kids, they all died.'

Larsen had almost forgotten the poliomyelitis outbreak of the 1950s, and the frantic search for a vaccine that would check the wildfire spread of a disease that could paralyse and kill. He recalled the tragedy of a young friend of his, a promising athlete crippled for life. Polio was caused by a virus that discriminated neither between sex nor race, yet how much more devastating must its impact have been up here, where there was little or no medical aid or attention. He began to understand better the fear of the group who had abandoned their comrade to die in this cave. He could also appreciate Umiak's irony about the progress of medical science. Thoughts of the dead man lying in the corner of the cave prompted another question. How come the corpse had remained unmolested by wild beasts?

'At the height of the fur trade whole regions were hunted out,' explained Umiak. 'I mean right out, cleared of everything that moved, either for meat or fur. It was a bonanza while it lasted, but it couldn't last long. A man might maintain a trap line a hundred and fifty miles long, and he had to get round it fast, before the wolverines and ravens beat him to it and robbed his traps. To do that he needed a large dog team, ten or more, and each dog needed seven pounds of meat or fish a day. You work that out in terms of salmon and caribou needed to last maybe six months of the year. Then suddenly the demand for furs fell. The hunters ate their dogs, and then starved themselves.'

'At least now you have oil to bring you an income,' ventured Larsen.

'For how long? We've seen the whalers come and go. We've seen the fur traders come and go. How long before the oil runs out, and the oil men go back where they came from? No, the only thing that endures up here is the land, the land and the sea and the harvests they yield. Then if the caribou don't come there are the seals, and if the seals stay out at sea there are walrus. In the spring the whales and the wild geese come, and in the summer the salmon swim up the rivers to spawn. In the fall the berries are ripe, and there are always the snowshoe hares, some years more than others.'

Larsen scarcely heard the end of this discourse. At the thought of caribou steaks sizzling on a bed of hot coals, of salmon curds, juicy and pink, peeling from the bone, goose flesh oozing rich fat, he began to salivate freely. A wave of nausea swept over him and for a moment he thought he was going to retch. Then hunger pains seized him in such a vice-like grip that he doubled up and fell forward, groaning and gasping for breath.

Umiak regarded him impassively. 'It doesn't do to talk about food in a situation like this,' he remarked reprovingly, as though the fault was all Larsen's. 'It doesn't even pay to think about it. I'll heat some water. It helps.'

It was, Larsen had to admit, better than nothing, and

he sipped the scalding water gratefully as beside him Umiak resumed work on the boots. 'How are your hands?' he asked suddenly.

Larsen studied them. The skin was chapped and raw, cracks had formed in the folds of his fingers and every knuckle had a running sore. Hitherto, in his mood of general misery, he had paid them scant regard, but now he was aware that he had difficulty even straightening his fingers. 'Rub some of this in,' ordered Umiak, pushing over the sealskin poke.

Holding his breath against the stench, Larsen did as he was bid. The relief was almost instantaneous, but at the same time he could not escape a qualm of fear, wondering what infection he might be introducing into his wounds.

It was time to move on. They had planned to take the caribou skins with them as protection against the cold, but already the hair was falling out in handfuls, and the ancient uncured hides cracked as they tried to roll them into a bundle small enough to transport on the sledge. In the end they left them in a pile as they had found them, laying the corpse of their guardian reverently back in place. They took the canteen, though, the knife, the flint and steel, and even the remains of the rancid oil.

As they prepared to leave, Umiak took off his own boots and pulled on the sealskin mukluks he had been working on earlier. 'They'd be too small to fit you,' he observed.

Larsen nodded. He was not sure whether he had received an apology or a mere statement of fact. 'Dead man's shoes,' he said softly, more to himself than to the other man.

'What was that?' asked Umiak.

'Oh, nothing,' said Larsen. 'I was merely thinking out loud.'

10

One after the other they crawled from the cave, Larsen leading, Umiak following behind. The light from the snow, lit by the early morning sun, blinded them momentarily, so they stood for a while, their backs to the sun, shading their eyes with their hands. The air was clean and cold after the mustiness of the cave, but there was no wind, and the dry chill was infinitely more bearable than mist and snow. Neither man looked down to where the snow outside the cave was scuffed and pock-marked by their footprints. So even Umiak failed to notice, just in front of the entrance, the deep and unmistakable paw print of a bear.

They set off up the defile, towards the saddle in the mountains. In the sunlight the peaks seemed flattened and shrunken against the sky. The saddle shimmered and danced in the distance, seeming to recede further and further away with every step they took. Larsen's legs felt like jelly, his bad leg burned and throbbed, yet he felt curiously alert and alive. After a while his head began to ache, and he wondered if it was the glare of the snow. He stopped to put on the snow goggles Umiak had made, but the headache persisted. It dawned on him then that he could be running a temperature.

There was nothing he could do about it, except press onward through the snow. The cable of the sledge bit into his shoulder, his boots grew heavier, the muscles of his legs seemed reluctant to obey the commands of his will, so that his feet refused to follow a straight line. Once he fell to his knees, and knelt there gasping for breath until his strength returned somewhat and he was able to go on.

The saddle was nearer now. Larsen did not dare to think what lay beyond, another mountain, a blind defile, an impassable cliff. Instead he concentrated on one step at a time, pausing when his strength threatened to forsake him altogether. Each time Umiak waited at his side without speaking, passive, immobile, seemingly disinterested in his plight. The man himself seemed indestructible, unaffected by the cold and hardship.

In fact Umiak himself was glad of the pauses to rest. Older than Larsen, he had noticed that in recent years he had begun to slow down, that the insidious onset of old age was creeping into his bones. He knew that Larsen was sick, but surmised it was merely weakness from his wound. He pondered the wisdom of returning to the cave, but guessed without asking that the other man would have none of it. He could only wait and if the time came when Larsen could go no further, he would load him on to the sledge and drag him back downhill.

A cold wind began to blow slantwise across their path, whipping up stinging flurries of frozen snow to add to their misery. He bent his shoulder to the towline of the sledge, taking as much of the strain off Larsen as he could, and plodded on. So at last they reached the summit of the pass.

Larsen lay face downwards in the snow, too exhausted to care. When at last he regained sufficient strength to walk the last few hundred yards through the pass and was able to look east beyond the ridge he was scarcely able to believe his eyes. A great wave of exultation and joy swept through him, a lump rose in his throat, and tears filled his eyes.

The mountain on which they stood sloped steeply away before them in one vast expanse of unbroken snow. At the foot lay a broad valley through which a wide river meandered north. To the east lay another pass, again wide and flat, with patches of scrub, orange and yellow and scarlet, showing above the snow. There was still a long way to go, but it seemed they were free of the mountains at last.

For a long while they rested there, their backs to a rock that shielded them from the wind, the sun shedding a faint but unmistakable warmth on their faces. Suddenly Umiak stiffened, and gripped Larsen's arm with such intensity that the pain jolted him awake. Umiak was on his feet, laughing and shaking his fists with delight, but at first Larsen was unable to make out why.

Then Umiak pointed, far up the valley to the north. Larsen could see nothing, only the river and the shimmering immensity of the snow-covered landscape. 'Caribou!' shouted Umiak and at last Larsen saw them, a ragged cluster of tiny black dots, strung out in the distance, moving with what appeared to be infinite slowness towards them. He guessed though that they were moving quite fast, and he tried, in vain, to estimate the distance that separated them. His heart sank at the realization that long before they could hope to make the descent of the mountain the caribou would be long gone, and he voiced his fears out loud.

Umiak's face fell. His exuberance subsided, and the two men gazed in silence at the prospect of their salvation passing beyond their reach. Then Larsen's eye fell on the sledge, the battered fragment of wing tip they had hauled so far. An idea came to mind, crazy, foolhardy in the extreme, but a risk that, in the circumstances, he was prepared to take. Umiak could please himself. Feverishly he began to untie the bundle of tattered carpet they still carried as bedding. 'We're going down the fast way,' he announced. 'Help me spread this on top of the sledge. We've no need to climb down the mountain. This time we ride.'

For a moment Umiak stared in horror, first at Larsen, and then at the steep smooth slope that stretched for over three thousand feet below them. There could be hidden rocks on which they would be broken to a pulp, uneven patches, hummocks of snow that would send them airborne. Their chances of staying with the sledge were almost nil. Then a slow smile spread over his face. This ride would be something to remember, if he survived. It beat whale hunting, it was better than driving a dog team flat out over rotten ice.

Larsen lay flat on the sledge, the towline wrapped round his mittened hands and wrists. Umiak lay on top, and he too took a hold of the cable. 'Ready?' asked Larsen, and Umiak grunted in reply.

For the first few yards the sledge ran slowly. Umiak's weight pressed down on Larsen, restricting his breathing so that he was forced to gasp for breath. Then suddenly, dramatically, the sledge speeded up. An icy chill froze Larsen's cheeks, and his eyes filled with tears so that he was almost blinded. A great roaring filled his ears, but whether it was the rush of blood to his head, the wind that whistled past or the passage of the sledge over the snow he could not be sure. At first gently, and then with increasing violence, the sledge began to pound. His teeth rattled, his eyes jerked in their sockets, his head banged against the sledge in spite of all he could do to control it. Above him Umiak's weight pounded and pummelled him, bruising his ribs until he thought they would break. Desperately he tried to breathe but, no matter how he tried, his chest refused to expand. His vision of the world turned red, and then there was only a roaring blackness into which, dimly, he was conscious he was falling.

He was shaving by a mountain stream. The lather was

ice cold, and the razor scraped roughly over his beard. Stranger still, the face mirrored in the waters of the pool, though familiar, was not his own. Then he woke, to find himself lying flat on his back, and Umiak was rubbing snow into his face. He wanted to ask how long he had lain unconscious, but when he tried to speak he couldn't. He could only lie there, feeling the Arctic air rasping into his labouring lungs, and the hammer of his heart pounding in his ears. At last he was able to sit up. 'Next time I ride on top,' he croaked, and Umiak grinned apologetically.

They looked back the way they had come, scarce able to believe they could have come unscathed down the mountainside, which now towered above them, seemingly sheer as a wall. The sledge had travelled a considerable distance across the level floor of the valley and close by they could hear the confused murmur of the river as it flowed north. Larsen's thoughts turned to the caribou, still heading towards them.

Umiak too was thinking hard. The caribou, he knew, were migrating south to their winter feeding grounds, but whether the group he had seen were the vanguard, or the last straggling members of a larger herd he could not be sure. Now they were down on the plain, dead ground hid the approaching deer from view, and mercifully the light wind blew from the north, so there was no fear that the caribou would be warned of his presence by scent.

All the same, the valley was wide. There was no cover from which to lay an ambush, and the snow covering was not yet deep enough for him to dig a trench in which to hide. In any case, to be sure of making a kill, he had to get close. He longed for a high-power rifle and a dozen of his own people, but it was useless to waste time speculating on such idle thoughts. He looked back up the valley, towards the south, vainly searching for some feature of the landscape that would serve his needs.

About half a mile upstream the river curved in a great meander. Here the valley narrowed somewhat, and he reasoned that if the deer maintained a straight course, as they usually did, they would cross the river rather than make the detour round it. If he could find some cover beneath the bank, he might bag one as they attempted to cross.

Leaving the sledge where it lay he set off upstream, calling to Larsen to follow. Larsen did his best, but in Umiak's eyes he was painfully slow. At last however they reached the first bend in the river, and stood on a wide gravel bar looking across to where the current had gouged away the further bank.

It was a likely place for the deer to cross. From the bank they could jump halfway across the stream, and from there it was an easy scramble up the bar. Spring floods had gouged a hollow in the bank, forming a place where with some difficulty a man might lie. However, first he had to cross the river. More important, he had to send Larsen over to the furthest point of the meander, so that if the deer threatened to circle round he could divert them back. It would require a nicety of timing and judgement that could only be expected of a skilled hunter. Umiak could only hope that Larsen's inexperience would not let them down.

First, though, he had to cross the river, a prospect he did not relish. Although he knew that the deer might arrive at any moment, he took the time to remove his boots and socks. He had no intention of risking frostbite by lying in sodden footwear. The icy water of the stream, though it rose no higher than his knees, swiftly rendered his feet devoid of all feeling, and it was a relief to gain the opposite bank, scrub his extremities dry, and plunge them back into the warmth of his boots.

Then there was nothing to do but wait, and wonder whether he had chosen the best site. He dared not raise his head above the bank, and Larsen was nowhere to be seen. His right hand gripped the revolver, nursing it inside the warmth of his parka. His left arm cradled his head. He lay without moving, listening, waiting, tension rising within him until he felt like a coiled spring. He knew that when he reacted, it would be with sudden violence, a force which always seemed to emanate from outside his being.

Meantime he listened, waiting for the low rumble, the steady clicking of hooves so characteristic of caribou. When at last it came it seemed, in the silence, to be far away over the valley towards Larsen. Bitter disappointment seized him, and then, far away, he heard Larsen shout, a long-drawn-out ululating wail that seemed to echo and re-echo from the mountains.

Then the rumble became a roar, a stampede that was on him almost before he could prepare himself for the onslaught. The caribou were upon him, coming not from the right or the left but directly over his head, in a flurry of black flying hooves that rained down snow and crumbling frozen earth into his face and eyes, temporarily blinding him and almost sending him rolling into the river.

He half rose to his knees. Three deer were already across the river. His left hand gripped his right wrist, his finger curled round the trigger of the gun. As one cow hit the water he fired at her head. He saw skin and hair and chips of white bone fly from her muzzle, but she only shook her head and scrambled on towards the opposite bank. He fired again, and this time she went down, kicking in the shallows. Another deer stood poised on the bank above him and he fired at the broad bulk of her side, just behind the shoulder, but at that very moment she sprang, and the bullet must have passed beneath her. Desperate, he fired again, saw the bullet strike water just below where her back showed above the surface. Then she was scrambling up the bank and galloping away, seemingly unscathed.

He had one shot left. Shaking now with panic and frustration he looked wildly round for a fresh target. Then to his horror he saw the first cow, the one he thought he had killed, get up, shake herself, and stagger towards the gravel bar. Suddenly he was ice cold, calm, and sure of himself. His last shot took her in the back of the head. She lurched up the bank, pulled herself clear of the water, and dropped dead. The gun was empty. Wearily he stared at it for a moment, and then dropped it in the river. Suddenly it had become just so much useless weight. There was no point carrying it any further.

11

A few miles up the valley a lone caribou took her last faltering steps and stood splay-legged in the snow, head hanging, flanks heaving as she strove to fill her lungs with air. The rest of the herd had left her far behind, and solitude brought uncomprehending fear.

She was the cow Umiak had fired at twice and thought he had missed. In fact his second shot, after entering the water, had caught her high in the chest, fragmenting itself on her rib, close to where it united with her spine, sending splinters of bone and crumbs of lead shooting like darts into lung and artery and vein. Now her lifeblood slowly leaked away. She felt no pain, only a hot wetness flowing inside her, and a growing weakness, a weariness that brought her to the verge of sleep. Daylight came and went to her failing sight like the slow beat of a bird's wings, so she did not sense the approach of the bear until a violent blow on her back sent her sprawling in the snow.

High above an eagle screamed, loud in the silence, and a raven huddled on a distant crag woke to instant alertness. Wings stiff spread it dropped from the cliff face, to be lifted skywards by a rising current of air. Its appearance aroused another of its kin, and so the message was semaphored across the vast open spaces of the tundra.

Far to the north the talebearers carried the news to a

wolf pack, lolling at their ease in a sheltered stand of stunted willow. With one accord they rose, and after milling round for a while in an excited disorganized fashion, set off at a steady swinging trot up river.

Larsen lay on the raw caribou hide Umiak had flayed from the dead cow. Every bone in his body felt as though it was broken. He breathed quickly, shallowly, trying not to expand his rib cage more than he needed to. His pulse raced, his head swam, and from time to time violent rigors shook his whole frame. Idly, almost detachedly, he wondered if he was going down with pneumonia.

Beside him Umiak sat hunched over the petrol stove, bone weary, tired beyond caring, too exhausted almost to stir the stew now simmering in the canteen. Earlier he had found Larsen sprawled face down in the snow, lying where he had fallen after his last frantic race to head the caribou in Umiak's direction, a drive that had proved almost too successful.

He had half carried, half dragged him to this bend in the river, where a low overhanging bluff gave some shelter from the wind, and a dry gravel bar, suitably hollowed, provided a comfortable place to lie. Then he had skinned and butchered the caribou, retrieved the sledge, and hauled the meat the few hundred yards to the camp site. He had abandoned the hooves and the entrails, feeling it was a waste, but one which he felt could not be helped, given the limitations on his time and strength. Even so, he had managed to salvage over a hundred pounds of meat and fat, including the head, together with a quart of blood.

Unknown to Larsen he had already fortified himself with several strips of raw liver, and the fat from behind the eyeballs, a prized delicacy he was sure Larsen would not appreciate. He justified what in other circumstances he would have regarded as an act of theft by the knowledge that one of them, at least, had to maintain his strength if either of them were to survive.

Now the stew was almost ready, the tongue, heart and some of the liver cut fine and boiled in river water. Golden globules of grease bubbled to the surface and shone glistening before his eyes, and the aroma of it was such that the saliva dribbled from his lips and his stomach churned in an agony of anticipation, so that it required all his will-power not to plunge his hand into the scalding liquid and help himself straightaway.

Even so his first act was to pour some of the soup into the lid of the vacuum flask and carry it across to Larsen, raise the man to a sitting position and fold the cup in his hands. Gratefully Larsen drained the cup and then sank back, his eyes closed, leaving Umiak to indulge in an orgy of eating.

Even then his mind was busy. He had seen the ravens gathering in the skies, but assumed that his kill was the focus of their attention. They were a familiar sight at every caribou hunt. He knew too that they were the constant companions and messengers of the wolves, and that sooner or later a wandering wolf pack would be drawn to the scene. Wolves posed no threat to his person, but he feared for the safety of their meat supply.

He was close to exhaustion, so weary he was falling asleep over his food. He knew he could not hope to keep watch all night, especially when he was full fed. Larsen, for the moment, could not help. He guessed they might have to rest up for several days, and even then they might not be able to continue their trek. So far the weather had held good, and such snowfalls as had heralded the onset of winter had been light, helping rather than hindering their progress. A heavy fall could render them prisoners, unable to move through the deep drifts.

Snow-shoes would help. Bitterly he reflected that it was years since he or anyone else had troubled to fashion a pair. It was so much easier to order them from a mail-order catalogue. He doubted if he could remember how to set about it now. In any case, it had traditionally been a long, leisurely task, occupying much of the summer, in spare moments when time hung heavy on a man's hands. It was immaterial. He could fashion rawhide webbing from the caribou skin, but he lacked the birch and willow to make the frames. Maybe he would find some further up the side stream he had noticed from the mountain top.

Then there was the question of fuel. The petrol supplies were running low. They might last another five days at most. Still, the river still flowed, though fringes of ice were forming along its banks, and they could survive perfectly well on raw meat.

He could eat no more. He roused Larsen and fed him again, noting with approval that the man fell once more into instant slumber. There was one more task to perform before he too could crawl to rest on that redolent couch. He found Larsen's fishing line, and set the caribou head, its antlers still attached, a little apart from the meat cache. He tied one end of the line to an antler, hung the empty canteen on the line so that it was suspended just above the stones that littered the river bank, and drew the line round the cache, fastening the other end to his foot. Anything approaching the meat in the night would break the line, tugging at his foot, and sending the canteen clattering against the stones. At least he hoped it would. It was the best he could do to safeguard their supplies. Now at last he could sleep, and gingerly, taking care not to disturb the fishing line or the slumbering Larsen, he crawled in beside him and sank into instant oblivion.

Larsen woke to full daylight, weak, but clear headed, and, for the first time he could remember since the crash, warm. The dense hollow hairs of the caribou skin spread beneath him in the hollow insulated him from the cold and enfolded him in a cosy nest. He still felt abominably stiff and sore, but at least he could breathe easily and the hunger pains had gone. Instead he was conscious of a raging thirst.

It was this that forced him at last, reluctantly, to abandon his couch, find the cup, and half stagger, half crawl to the edge of the stream. It was only then, after he had drunk two cupfuls, that he missed Umiak. He gazed around him, at the meat cache, now rimed with hoarfrost, at the litter of the camp site, and finally, at the surrounding countryside.

It was empty. So it had come to this then. Umiak had abandoned him, left him with food and water and a bed, to survive or die in the wilderness, just like the man in the cave. Yet it seemed he had taken nothing for himself, and not even Umiak could survive without the barest essentials. Maybe he was ashamed, humiliated by his poor performance with the gun the day before. Maybe he had simply walked off to die. Or maybe he had met with an accident, was lying dead or injured somewhere.

Suddenly he could stand the solitude and silence no more. '*Umiak*,' he yelled. '*Umiaaak*.' The echoes came back from the mountains, mocking him in his plight, but no answering call came from Umiak. He fell to his knees beside the water, gazing into the black waters of the pool. His reflection stared back, haggard-eyed, gaunt-cheeked, fringed with the beginnings of a straggly blond beard, the face of a stranger, haunted, Christlike.

Suddenly he began to laugh softly to himself. Though raised in a community of strict Presbyterian belief, he had never been himself a particularly religious man, and scenes he had witnessed later in life had raised in him doubts about the very existence of God. Yet belief persisted, so that now he saw the huge irony of the joke. 'Christ,' he said, 'if you died to save me from my sins, you wasted your time. I'm going to die here, in this wilderness your father created. For what? For the wolves? The bears? The caribou? Certainly not for me. Or am I no more important than they?'

The reflection grinned back at him, teeth bared, wolfish, and suddenly he picked up a stone and flung it into the water, shattering the image. Abruptly he turned away, still laughing, and hobbled back up the beach. He bethought himself to cook some of the caribou meat, but he did not feel particularly hungry. He ought, he knew, to change the dressing on his leg, but he was too apathetic to care. So he sat hunched on the river bank, staring north down the valley, at the featureless frozen landscape.

In the distance a dark shape materialized against the snow, emerging from a hidden dip in the ground. It was Umiak for sure, and, suddenly elated, Larsen leaped to his feet, waving his arms above his head. Then, as he watched, and the figure gave no answering wave, he realized his mistake. It was no man, but a lone caribou, trekking its way south to join the rest of its kind. If Umiak had not been so trigger-happy, he might have bagged this one too. At least its hide would be useful. Then he looked again, and saw that it was indeed Umiak, plodding steadily along, and bent under a huge burden of dry slender twigs.

Larsen limped forward to meet him and help relieve him of his burden. Umiak straightened his back with a grunt, and for the first time Larsen noticed the fatigue and strain etched in the older man's face. 'You've been busy,' he commented. 'Good job somebody's prepared to get up and work around here, instead of lying sleeping all day.'

Umiak grinned. 'I hoped you might sleep longer. You needed the rest.'

'I slept well,' said Larsen. 'That caribou hide makes a luxurious bed.'

'Nothing but the best is good enough for our guests,'

said Umiak solemnly, and they both laughed. 'Why didn't you stay there?'

'I woke thirsty,' replied Larsen, 'and then when I found you were missing...'

'You thought I'd deserted you maybe?' queried Umiak.

'Oh no! It wasn't that...' protested Larsen, and then he hesitated. 'Well, to be honest, it did cross my mind, but then I thought you'd more likely gone off exploring, and then I began to worry in case you'd got lost or met with an accident...' He broke off, aware that he was babbling, and that Umiak was watching him intently.

'I was at fault,' admitted Umiak. 'I should not have gone off and left you. We make a pact, eh? From now on neither of us leaves the other without saying where we are going and why. It's wisest, and I should have thought.'

'I'll shake hands on that,' said Larsen. Suddenly he felt hungry.

An hour later both men sat replete. They had each eaten about a pound of fat caribou steak apiece, grilled in the hot embers of the fire, and a canteen full of water stood heating in front of them. 'Coffee would be nice,' murmured Larsen.

'Tea I can offer you,' said Umiak. 'Labrador tea.' He picked up a bundle of herbs he had brought back with the sticks, stripped the leaves from a sprig, and dropped them into the vacuum flask. Then he added water from the canteen. Larsen sipped the brew gingerly. It was strongly aromatic, almost antiseptic in taste, but warming and stimulating to the palate. He decided he liked it, and drained the cup before passing it to Umiak.

'You know,' he said dreamily. 'I'm beginning to think that when the hunting was good, your people lived pretty high off the hog, if you understand the expression. Oh, I don't mean you had it easy, but you had the best.'

Umiak sat silent for a while, trying to quell the rancour that rose in him like bile, reminding himself that this white man was like all the rest, unable to understand or appreciate the glory that once had been. Yet he was beginning to, and it was important that he should understand fully, if the future was to unite the best of both worlds.

'Life was easy, and life was hard,' he began. 'If a hunter woke in the morning and heard the wind blowing strong off the land, he knew it was pointless going out on the ice, because the seals would be far out to sea. So he might be idle for a week or more. But when the weather was right, then the hunt took precedence over everything. He might wait a day for a seal to show, but then, if he killed a big one, say an *oogruk*, a bearded seal, it might weigh five hundred pounds or more, and then he was faced with the job of getting it on the sledge and dragging it four or five miles over the ice. That was hard work.

'The wilderness provides, and we take only the best. Fat caribou calves, not stringy cows or bulls stinking of the rut. When the salmon are running, for a fortnight we might work eighteen hours a day. We keep the king salmon for ourselves and feed the chum salmon to our dogs. Once we slept on the softest of skins, our wives wore a ransom in fine furs, and even in the coldest weather caribou skins are too warm to work in. We harvest the berries in late summer, and the salmon berries are best. Even today we will not sell them, although we can ask any price we like for them. We will give them as a gift, but only to a special friend. Sometimes a family will charter a plane, just to fly out to the berry grounds. Life was good, and we were happy. It will be good again for my people, just so long as we can retain our traditional rights.'

He paused and chuckled. 'A wise man said, and he was a white man, "An Indian hunts to live, but an Eskimo lives to hunt." That is very true I think.'

'But isn't there a danger,' queried Larsen, 'that you may exhaust the wealth that the wilderness has to offer? After all, I've heard your people starved in the past.'

Umiak nodded sombrely. 'It is true. My people were thoughtless and wasteful at times. First the whalers paid us to hunt for them. We killed the great whales, just for the baleen, and left much meat to rot. We killed caribou, too, more than we needed, to supply meat to the whalers and the fur traders. And of course we sold furs, rather than just trap what we needed for ourselves.'

He sighed, remembering. 'So we must have restrictions, and some people will resist. So we must be sure that those restraints on our hunting are ones we decide and agree upon, not those imposed on us by white men who do not understand our ways.'

'And in return, what do you offer?' asked Larsen.

'We have already given much. We have given land, land that was ours for ten thousand years. We offer its mineral resources, at a fair price. We offer our labour. One day perhaps we may have to sacrifice our land and our lives in your defence.'

Suddenly Larsen remembered that the vast might of Russia lay just beyond the Pole, sprawled across nearly half the northern hemisphere, and nearer than his own home in the States. He shuddered at the thought. 'Here's one white man who hopes you never have to make that sacrifice,' he murmured.

'That is why we try to make your armed forces welcome,' replied Umiak. 'Especially some of our young ladies.'

'Some of them are very beautiful,' observed Larsen, remembering the girl in the bar.

'The soldiers, or the ladies?' asked Umiak, and they both laughed, two middle-aged men slipping into an easy familiarity, cementing the first bonds of a fragile friendship that knew no barriers of race or creed.

'We ought to move on, if you can make it,' said Umiak. 'There's a good camp site about a mile up the valley. There's a rock overhang by a waterfall, and scrub willow and poplar growing above the fall. Plenty of dry timber, and berries too. We could rest up there a couple of days, eat and get strong, and we should still have enough meat to last us the remainder of the trip.'

Despite his weakness, Larsen was all for moving off at once, but Umiak was not disposed to hurry. The exertions of the previous day had tired him more than he cared to admit, and already, while Larsen had slept, he had tramped a good six miles, half that distance with a load of wood on his back. Already that supply was almost consumed by the flames of their fire. 'There's no hurry,' he muttered, 'I'm going to rest awhile. Why don't you play with that fishing rod of yours? There's sure to be a fish in that pool.'

So saying he lay back on the bedding and in a few moments he was asleep. Larsen shrugged resignedly and began to assemble his tackle. Then he walked stiffly to the head of the pool, flicked a small gold spinner across to the deep water under the far bank, waited a moment and began to retrieve.

Immediately he was, as usual, wholly absorbed in his occupation, and his third cast brought a sudden savage strike. His rod bent double, and seconds later a grayling of about a pound was flapping on the bank. Two casts later he caught a second one about the same weight. There came a lull, and then his rod bent into a heavier, stronger fish, which made several fast runs down the pool and bored deep before turning on its side exhausted. It was a char, deep-flanked and red-bellied, at least three pounds in weight.

For a time he fished on, systematically working his way down the pool, but no more fish came, although he changed his lure several times. At last he picked up his catch and walked the few yards back to camp. Umiak still slept, so he hung the fish on the antlers of the caribou and then he too stretched himself on the ground to sleep.

12

The site Umiak had found was, in comparison to earlier camps, the last word in luxury. They spread the caribou hide over a thick bed of springy twigs and moss, beneath a sloping sandstone slab that gave them shelter from the weather. Dry brushwood, willow and alder, lined the banks of the stream where it had been deposited by spring floods, and soon they had a bright fire of small sticks glowing among the stones. The polished underside of the sledge acted as a reflector to the flames, throwing the heat back into the shelter. They had meat, fish and berries in plenty, but Larsen was in a bad way.

The effort of dragging the heavily laden sledge the few miles down the valley had taxed him severely. He had no appetite, only a raging thirst, and his flushed appearance indicated a rapidly rising temperature. His leg throbbed and burned, and when he removed the bandages both men saw that a fresh abscess was forming. The skin was red and swollen, bulging ominously below the site of the earlier wound, fiery to the touch.

Umiak put fresh water in the canteen and set it to warm in the flames. Then he got a pad of cloth, and as soon as he judged the water hot enough for Larsen to bear he began applying poultices to the wound. If anything they made the pain worse, and for over an hour

Larsen lay gritting his teeth, trying to strangle a desire to scream out loud. At last he reached into his pocket and pulled out his little penknife. 'Cut it,' he gasped. 'Let the poison out.'

Umiak took the knife, opened the smallest blade, and tested the edge with his thumb. It was razor sharp. Without hesitating, without giving Larsen time to reconsider, or even prepare himself for the shock, he plunged the point of the knife deep into the abscess and cut downwards. Then Larsen did scream, as thick yellow pus streaked with thin red stripes of blood spurted out of the wound.

'All over,' said Umiak, glancing at his patient, but Larsen had fainted dead away, and Umiak took full advantage of the fact to irrigate the abscess thoroughly with warm water. Then he gazed at the wound critically. A clean two-inch slash bled freely below the abscess, and he wondered if perhaps he had opened it too wide. He decided not. He did not want the incision to heal over before the deep-seated infection cleared, otherwise the abscess would re-form.

He thought of packing the cavity with a strip of cloth, but then he had a better idea. Willow grew in profusion along the river bank, and he remembered his mother using the bark as a dressing. Swiftly he gathered a handful of young shoots, stripped the bark from them, and shredded it into the canteen along with a cupful of water, boiling the whole concoction into a sloppy mush. By the time it had cooled and he had decanted the liquid from the bark, Larsen had recovered. He made no murmur of protest as Umiak gently packed the wound with the willow bark paste and bound up his leg, but he resisted violently when Umiak tried to get him to drink the bitter juice. Finally he threw it back at a gulp, and though he retched violently, he kept it down. Shortly after his fever seemed to abate until at last he fell into a deep sleep.

That night the wolves came. Umiak heard them quarrelling over the caribou entrails further up the valley, but he knew that those few frozen remains would not sustain them for long. Shortly after he caught the glint of a pair of green eyes glowing in the darkness beyond the fire, and he lobbed a rock in their direction. The twin lights went out, but though he could neither see nor hear the wolves he knew they were all around. So he sat wakeful, keeping the fire bright, guarding the precious cache of meat which he knew would disappear in minutes if once he fell asleep. Beside him Larsen stirred fretfully from time to time, but he did not wake.

The long hours passed and the stars moved in remorseless procession across the cloudless sky. From time to time Umiak threw another stick on the blaze, keeping the tiniest of flames flickering in the night, sitting hunched over the fire in order to gain the maximum benefit from the heat. Despite himself he began to nod and doze, to enjoy brief intervals of merciful oblivion. Each time the watching wolves moved closer, only to scatter as he jerked upright and pelted them with stones.

He took a long slender willow stick and sharpened one end to a point. Thereafter he sat with the blunt end of the stick resting on the stones and the point under his chin, so that each time he dozed the pinprick of pain jolted him awake. Morning would come, and with the daylight the wolves would depart. Then he could sleep.

There was no chance of them moving on for at least a day or so. They both needed rest, and Larsen's leg needed time to heal, if it was ever going to. He seriously doubted whether they could continue their journey and transport the food they needed to sustain them on the trip. Yet without adequate rations they could not hope to survive.

They could cut some of the meat into strips and dry it, perhaps smoke some of it over the fire. This would reduce the bulk and weight, and mixed with berries it would provide sufficient nourishment. Meanwhile it would pay to eat as much as they could, always assuming Larsen felt well enough to eat. He had long since lost all reckoning of how far they had travelled, but guessed they still had far to go. Winter had not even begun to bite with the ferocity to which he was accustomed. He could only pray that the weather would hold.

Larsen woke weak but refreshed, and eager for his share of the fish Umiak had poached in the canteen. His wound, when they inspected it, was looking cleaner and healthier, and much of the swelling and inflammation had died down. The willow bark treatment seemed to be working, so they repeated it, but when Larsen tried to stand he found his leg could scarcely bear his weight, so he rested while Umiak dried meat and harvested berries from the hill.

Most of the day they spent sleeping and eating, so that when night came they were both wakeful and ready for the wolves. They heard them howling as the long Arctic twilight began to fall, and twice they glimpsed a dim grey shape moving on the far side of the stream. Umiak had collected a goodly store of firewood, and between them they kept the flames of their fire flickering through the darkness. Umiak had impressed on Larsen the need to conserve fuel. Even so Larsen was astounded at the way the fire devoured the thin dry sticks, and in spite of their care the wood-pile diminished rapidly as the long hours passed. Already they had gleaned every scrap of wood from the immediate vicinity of the site. Umiak explained that the continuing quest for fuel was one of the prime influences on the nomadic way of life.

From time to time they discouraged the wolves by pelting them with stones, and once Larsen was rewarded by the satisfaction of hearing an anguished yelp as he scored a direct hit. Yet it seemed that in spite of their efforts the pack was growing bolder, and although Umiak assured him that they presented no real threat Larsen found himself wondering rather nervously how he would react if he was alone. Tentatively he asked Umiak how he would feel.

Umiak thought a while before replying. 'It is not good for a man to live alone,' he said. 'I have known trappers, living alone in the wilds for weeks on end, but they become strange in their ways. Two men can get along, but they have to be very good friends, lifelong friends, otherwise, sooner or later, they fall out. Three men together mean trouble. Two of them always gang up on the third, until the knives are out.'

He laughed, and threw another twig on the fire, watching the yellow flames leap into life. 'Sometimes I think we are just like those wolves out there, pack animals, needing each other in order to function best. A man is respected not because he is a good hunter, but because he is a good hunter that shares. A man who keeps his meat to himself is hated and despised. I knew of a man once who had travelled south and learned the white man's ways. When he returned he set up a store in his village so he could sell the goods his people needed. Within a month he was out of business. He had given away or loaned all the goods in his store. He did not suffer or starve though. Everyone brought him presents, even returning some of the goods he had given away. He gave up shopkeeping after that and became a hunter like the rest.'

Larsen pondered this a while. 'But you own a whaling boat,' he said.

'True,' replied Umiak. 'As did my father before me, but I do not own the whales we catch. Each one is shared, divided according to ancient custom, and my crew only sail with me because I am lucky in finding the whale. If I wasn't, or failed to share the catch, my crew would desert me, and my boat would be of no more use.'

A sudden outburst of snarling as the wolves quarrelled amongst themselves interrupted him and he heaved another rock in their general direction. In the silence that followed he laughed softly. 'Man and wolf, my friend, pack animals alike, hunting the same quarry over the same land, timid when alone, braver when in company. Yet the wolf has always feared man, probably for the simple reason that man has learned to throw stones. The wolf never will. His paws are the wrong shape.'

It was Larsen's turn to laugh then, partly at the ludicrous notion of a wolf pack throwing stones, and partly at the sheer incongruity of their situation, sitting in the middle of nowhere, guarding a pile of raw caribou flesh, and conversing as naturally as two men enjoying a drink in a downtown bar. All the same, he could not repress a shudder at the thought of lying alone beside a dying camp-fire, surrounded by a pack of hungry wolves. There was much truth in Umiak's words. Man and wolf were alike, almost mirror images of each other. Yet, in spite of all, man did fear the wolf.

Again Umiak displayed that uncanny knack of seeming to read his thoughts. 'It is what man imagines the wolf to be that makes him afraid, rather than what the wolf is.'

The wolves showed no sign of venturing closer. The long night passed, and Larsen was beginning to doze, when suddenly, far out across the empty expanse of the tundra there came the deep, long drawn-out howl of another wolf. There was an outburst of excitement among the waiting pack, a flurry of barking and a glimpse of fleeting bodies. Next moment the two men were alone under the empty sky and the stars.

Larsen lay wakeful for a while, but the wolf pack did not return. Finally he fell asleep, but Umiak sat on, his eyes glittering in the firelight, his hunched figure so still it might have been carved from stone. Despite what he had said he knew that there were outstanding differences between wolf and man, in the wolf's favour. The wolf was more successful in its lifestyle, more at home, more at one with the wilderness than even his own people. From the very beginning the wolf had been better-equipped for survival. He could better endure the cold and the long periods of fasting and possessed the stamina to travel vast distances without apparent effort. And, it occurred to Umiak, his ancestors had been more at home in the wilderness than he was. Now he felt like a man standing between two worlds, unwilling to enter one, unable to turn back to the other. Either way, the future seemed uncertain and dark.

The night was almost over. Dawn was yet a long way off, but already the darkness had lessened, giving form and shape to the surrounding rocks and bushes. Umiak's head drooped in sleep. Once he roused, stiff and cold, and felt around for another stick to add to the dying fire. There were none left. They had used the last of their supply.

His hand dropped in his lap as slumber overtook him once more. At that moment the wolves returned. Their encounter with the other wolf pack had been brief and decisive. Stronger, greater in number, they had driven the alien wolves away from what they considered their territory by a short and bloodless display of ferocity. Now they were back to reclaim what they regarded as their rightful prey.

Larsen woke, struggling to surface from deep slumber, to hear Umiak yelling and screaming and throwing stones in all directions. The night seemed filled with fleeting grey shapes. One actually brushed against him as he sat up and flung aside the carpet that covered him. He looked in the direction of the meat cache, and it seemed in the gloom to be writhing with new life. He too began to yell and to heave rocks at random, but almost before he had begun it seemed that the raid was over. The wolf pack vanished as swiftly as it had appeared, and Umiak stood at his side, trembling and cursing violently, at the wolves and at himself.

Together they crossed the few yards of gravel to what remained of the meat cache. Only the hindquarters remained. 'I made it too easy for them,' Umiak muttered angrily. 'If only I'd thought. If only I'd left the carcase intact. Instead I butchered it up into easily manageable chunks, so all they had to do was pick up a lump of meat apiece and carry it off.'

'You weren't to know – ' began Larsen.

'That's just the point,' complained Umiak. 'I should have known. I should have thought. At least they left the hindquarters. It's a good job I didn't have an axe, otherwise I would have divided them too, and they would have gone. I should have thought,' he reproached himself again. 'A man can't make too many mistakes like that in the wilderness and hope to survive.'

'Well,' remarked Larsen, 'at least the problem of how to carry the meat has been solved for us. And we've still got the meat we dried, and the berries, and the hindquarters. We could be worse off... Besides,' he added peering into the gloom, 'by the looks of things, we've got wolf meat to add to the pot.'

The darkness hid Umiak's expression as he regarded Larsen with renewed interest and respect. Here was one white man, it seemed, who was learning to live with the wild. Together they walked over to where a half-grown wolf lay sprawled on the ground. One of their stones must have scored a lucky hit, striking the wolf on the side of the head. One eye had been crushed to a pulp, and blood still trickled from its ear. Gingerly Umiak took hold of its tail and dragged it a foot or so across the ground. More than one man, he knew, had been badly bitten by an apparently dead wolf. This one though was quite dead, and they carried it back to the fire.

'You know,' said Umiak wonderingly, 'I've never tasted wolf.'

By tacit consent they mixed some of the wolf meat with a caribou stew, but they both found it to be quite palatable. Umiak was not unduly surprised. 'Lots of things are good to eat, if people would only try them. Porcupine, for instance, and lynx. Lynx meat is delicious, especially if the cat has fed on lots of rabbit. Fox is good too, but few people eat them now. This meat is a bit like fox.' Suddenly he chuckled quietly and looked at Larsen, a hint of mischief in his eye. 'There's an old belief among my people that a man who eats wolf meat will father unruly, destructive children, just like wolves.'

Larsen grinned ruefully. 'There's nothing I'd like better than to put your theory to the test. Meantime I'll just concentrate on staying alive. What do you think? Do we move on?'

'There's nothing to keep us here,' admitted Umiak. 'We ought to make the effort while the food lasts. We may get lucky further on, but we can't depend on it. How's the leg?'

'Feels good,' said Larsen. 'I'll change the dressing in a minute.'

The wound looked clean and healthy and after it was re-dressed it gave him little discomfort, even when he put his full weight on the leg. They set about breaking camp and loading the sledge. The caribou hide seemed less malodorous to Larsen, or maybe he was just getting used to the smell. They had been careful to spread it fur side down to dry and air in the crisp Arctic wind, and it showed no sign of mouldering or decay. Larsen looked at the wolf skin Umiak had draped over a rock. For the first time the full beauty and richness of the fur, black and pale tan and grey, with the long guard hairs frosted with silver, struck him with a force like a blow, so that he almost regretted the death of the wolf. 'I wonder which one of us threw the stone that killed it?' he asked.

Umiak looked at him sharply. 'Does it matter?' he queried.

Larsen couldn't answer. It had occurred to him that the pelt would make a hat for Sylvie, with maybe a collar and gloves to match, and then maybe she would give him some unruly and destructive children. The intensity of feeling this evoked almost overwhelmed him, and once again he was astonished at the ease with which sudden emotion could break down his self-control. The wilderness seemed to have that effect on a guy, he thought, almost as if he were maudlin drunk.

'Keep the pelt if you want it,' said Umiak off-handedly. 'It might just as easily have been your stone as mine.'

Larsen muttered his thanks. Again he couldn't escape the feeling that Umiak had read his mind.

By late morning they were ready to move on. The sledge felt heavier now, but the going was good, the air was calm, and a slight haze cut the glare of the sun as it hung low on the horizon. The way ahead sloped gently upwards, following a series of gentle rises and hills. They moved slowly but steadily, pausing occasionally to rest before leaning their weight into the towline once more. Neither man knew that they were heading once more into the mountains. Nor were they aware that if they had turned south and headed a few miles up the main river valley, they would have come to not one but two cabins, offering warmth and shelter against the coming winter. With their meat gone, it wouldn't have mattered anyhow. Last, but by no means least, Umiak had been wrong about the bear.

13

Here and there across the icy wastes of the Arctic wilderness, scattered over the barren rock screes of some forgotten mountain-side, or buried beneath a soft carpet of mosses and fern, lie a few shattered fragments of bone. They are all that remain of men who have died in the mistaken belief that grizzly bears can neither climb trees nor jump.

Still the twin myths persisted, and Umiak, in spite of his experience, was a firm believer in both. So he had dismissed the threat of the bear, convinced they had left it far behind. In fact he was not so very far away, nosing round the camp site they had left earlier that morning. He had crossed the chasm with ease, and found an easier way down off the mountain.

There in the valley he had found the caribou dying from the gunshot wounds earlier inflicted by Umiak and gorged until he was full. Throughout that day he had lain resting, tolerating the ravens that came and shredded the carcase of meat, but driving away a pair of wolverines that came to share the feast. During the night they tried again and, despite his angry rushes, succeeded in bearing away a substantial portion of the prize. By the end of the second day the grizzly was reduced to cracking bones for the marrow.

Hair torn out by the ravens lay spread over the snow,

now pink-tinged and strewn with minute scraps of frozen flesh. The remainder of the carcase seemed to have settled into the earth. Only the skull, with one antler still attached, lay lopsidedly among the stones.

Gradually the bear lost interest in the remains. His taste was for hot meat, fresh with the flavour of blood and salt, or better still sweet with the savour of corruption. Full fed, he wandered down to the river, drank some of the icy water, and moved slowly downstream.

His mantle of snow had grown thicker. Long icicles, yellowed by dirt from his pelt, hung down his flanks. His muzzle and chest were stained red, as were his paws. Only his massive head was free of snow, and his small eyes glittered dark in the sun. He lingered long at the camp site, finding much to occupy his attention, scraps of caribou bone and sinew, fish heads, and the remains of the wolf, stripped of most of its flesh. His nose told him more as he explored the odours lingering among the stones, evoking memories of the corpse he had dragged from its cairn of stones. The same scent led him away up the valley, following in the wake of the two men.

As the day wore on the early morning haze thickened, and as they climbed steadily higher mist began to develop. Soon the two men were blanketed in thick fog, dark and chill, swirling down from the hills and enveloping them in fine beads of moisture that froze in the icy wind, riming their clothing, their eyebrows and hair. Despite their exertion the cold seemed to penetrate through to their skin, a raw, damp cold that seemed to chill them far more than the dry sub-zero temperatures they had experienced for the past few days. To try to get warm they increased their pace, but after a while weakness and exhaustion forced them to slow down.

The snow lay deeper here, swept into drifts in which they floundered up to their knees. At first it was fine and powdery, but gradually the freezing fog began to form an ice crust on the surface of the snow, a thin brittle film through which their feet broke at every stride. They plodded on, step after slow careful step, ever aware that the ground was still rising before them. The cloud obscured their vision, enveloped them in a silence so profound that the faint rasp of their breathing seemed unnaturally harsh and loud. They had to strain their ears to catch the faint muffled murmur of the stream beside them. Neither man spoke, instead saving what little energy he could muster simply to keep upright and keep moving.

Now the ground began to rise more steeply. From time to time, when the mist cleared a little, they caught shadowy glimpses of rocky crags on their right. The way became more treacherous and uneven, and Umiak knew that neither of them could carry on much further without a break. There was no fuel or shelter as far as he could see. They had left the willow thickets far behind, and the stream, whenever they passed close to it, flowed ice-rimmed over the bare stones.

Then quite suddenly they broke through the blanket of cloud, and both men stopped in their tracks. Larsen felt a lurch of fear and dismay as he surveyed the scene before them. On all sides the mountains closed in like a wall. The valley lay in deep shadow, and what little sky they could see was a deep blue. Somewhere on their right the sun shone, hidden by a high rampart of snow-covered rock. Ahead the stream divided, and without a word the two men made their way to the fork.

Here a massive buttress of stone reared its bulk against the mountainside, towering thirty feet above the stream at its base. Here the water foamed through a narrow channel carved into the solid rock, but there was a ledge, slippery with ice and frozen snow, along which they could pass. They navigated it cautiously, knowing that one slip could be fatal.

Beyond the valley opened up into a small glen. Larsen

eased himself from under the towline of the sledge and sank down on to a rock. 'Which way now?' he grunted.

'No way for now,' replied Umiak. 'First we rest, eat, drink and regain our strength.'

At least they had plenty of food, and they ate well, for, as Umiak pointed out, there was no sense in rationing themselves to the point where they were too weak to travel. That would only delay the inevitable outcome of death by starvation. Far better to stay strong, and let the future take care of itself. Larsen, who was ravenous, found no quarrel with this logic.

They had taken the precaution of boiling thick caribou steaks before they left camp. That the meat was now cold, that the gravy, thickened with blood and berries, was greasy and congealed with fat, no longer troubled Larsen. His hands were blackened with charcoal and grimed with dirt, and Umiak's were just as bad, but they each dipped into the plastic bag that held the stew without a qualm, so that before the end of the meal their fingers were cleaner than when they had started.

Larsen's clothes stank. His whole body crawled as warmth began to flow back into his limbs. His straggly beard itched and his hair was tangled and unkempt. Above all, now that he was full fed, he longed for a hot steaming bath, a slow luxurious scraping away of the grime that he felt encased him like a crustacean's shell. Then the comfort of a clean bed, and the softness of a pillow on which to lay his head. He sat back and rested his head against the unyielding surface of the rock. He felt he could sleep for a week.

His eyelids drooped and he fell into a doze, leaving Umiak alone with his own thoughts. He still blamed himself for the loss of the caribou meat. Had he not been so busy with the knife, had he not butchered the carcase so efficiently, cutting it into easily manageable joints, the wolves might have got away with a bite or two, but no more.

Whether they could have hauled the meat this far, even assuming they had saved it, was another matter. He had himself pulled heavier loads, over greater distances, but that had been when he was young and strong. Now he felt old, and desperately weary, yet he knew they must go on, for with each passing day their chances of survival grew less. As the nights grew longer, the cold deepened and the weather grew worse.

Now they were faced with another imponderable. He sat staring at the twin watercourses flowing down out of the mountains. Which one, if either, would lead them out of the mountains, or would they have to retrace their steps and make their way back to the camp site they had left?

The day was well spent. It seemed futile to spend the rest of it toiling up what might prove to be a blind alley, and the more rest Larsen got now the better he would be able to face the journey ahead. Meanwhile there were worse places to spend the night. The valley was sheltered, and it was warmer up here in the mountains than in the plains below. It was in the lowlands that the intense cold settled. He would leave Larsen here and explore one stream. If that route proved impassable he would try the other, leaving Larsen to unload the sledge and make preparations for the night.

Once the decision was made he felt better. His weariness and depression fell away, and rousing Larsen, he told him of his plans. At first Larsen demurred, volunteering to take one route while Umiak explored the other, but as Umiak pointed out, that would mean leaving their food supply unguarded. Convinced, Larsen watched him depart, picking his way among the ice-covered boulders that lay strewn alongside the river-bed. Gradually his figure grew smaller, then vanished behind the shoulder of the hill.

Larsen closed his eyes and sank back against the boulder, but the warm drowsiness had deserted him. He felt alert and aware, and conscious of the chill of inertia. He stood up and wandered around, slapping his arms across his chest in an effort to restore his circulation, casting his eye around in search of a suitable spot to spend the night. There seemed none better than the flat space beneath the rock against which he had been leaning, so he unstrapped the bedding from the sledge and spread it on the ground.

That done he sat down again and tried to relax, but found he could not. The silence of the wilderness overwhelmed him and enveloped him like a shroud, a stillness broken only by the confused murmuring of the stream as it flowed at his feet. It was like a conversation half heard but unintelligible, and as he listened it seemed to grow louder so that he became irritated and threw a stone into the ripples, merely for the satisfaction of hearing the splash.

About fifty yards below him, just above the point where the river narrowed into a foaming channel cut deep into the rock, it widened out into a small pool. Larsen fell to wondering if it held any fish. It seemed unlikely, but he had caught trout high in the mountains before in just such streams as this. That had been in summer though, when the waters were high with snow melt after the spring thaw and flies were hatching in the warm sun.

This river was sunken and low, its waters fringed with ice along the margins, the surface of the pool mirror-calm and black in the shadow of the hill. The conditions were far from perfect, but what after all did he have to lose? He had no fly tackle as such, only his spinning rod, and a fixed spool reel loaded with nylon monofilament line. Still, he had a small plastic bubble float and a selection of flies, and he had long ago mastered the technique of attaching a fly on a long trace below the bubble float and letting the tackle drift downstream with the current. It was hardly fly fishing as such, but one way of taking fish. At least it was better than sitting brooding, letting the wilderness get under his skin.

Soon the tiny plastic bubble was meandering gently down the pool, drifting with the current, but all the while held gently in check by the pressure of Larsen's finger on the line as it unwound itself from the spool. The first run down produced nothing. Nor did the second, but on the third run Larsen varied his technique by letting the float down in a series of jerks. Stopping the float made the fly rise to the surface, and halfway down he was rewarded by a slashing take and a series of jerks as a trout went skidding slantwise across the pool.

Fish came steadily after that, not every time but often enough to keep Larsen interested and absorbed. The trout were small, no more than a few ounces in weight, but perfectly formed and fighting fit. Soon five lay in a neat row on an icy slab of rock, their colours fading as they dried in the cold air.

Suddenly the fish stopped coming to the fly. Still Larsen fished on, his anxiety mounting as time passed and he still failed to add a sixth fish to his catch. Never before, in all the years he had spent fishing, in rivers and streams and lakes in various parts of the world, could he remember when he so desperately wanted to catch just one more fish. Five lay on the stone. One more would mean three each, fried in caribou fat before the main meal. That they would amount to no more than a few mouthfuls each was irrelevant. Unconsciously, he had reverted back to his ancient role as a hunter, and so he fished on, his whole concentration fixed on the tiny plastic bubble that bobbed its way down the icy black water of the pool. His foot slipped on a boulder, jarring his bad leg and making him wince with pain, but he ignored it, his whole being intent on getting that last fish before Umiak returned.

So he did not notice that far down the river the landscape moved. An ice-clad boulder, indistinguishable from a hundred others that littered the banks of the stream gradually elongated and grew, rearing up until it was an eight-foot monolith against the sky. Then it sank down again, and drifted slowly, almost imperceptibly across the river and up the side of the hill.

Far away up the valley, Umiak stood looking reflectively up at a tangled wall of jagged boulders and splinters of rock, bound in a shroud of ice from which, at the base, the headwaters of the stream oozed out. Almost tenderly, he laid his hand on one of the stones. It fell away at his touch, bringing several more in its wake, and Umiak stepped back hurriedly as the whole mass seemed to shift and stir. The entire wall, towering thirty feet above his head, was poised on the brink of collapse. Later the cold of winter would encase it in bands harder than iron, but right now any slight disturbance, a sudden gust of wind, even a loud shout, would bring untold thousands of tons of rock and ice and silt crashing down in a great wave. There was no way on from here.

Softly he moved away from the menacing barricade that towered above him, retracing his steps back downstream. After a few yards he stopped and sat down on a flat slab of rock. The light was fading, the dusting of snow on the mountain-side turning to grey as the shadows lengthened. He knew he should not linger, yet he felt a strange reluctance to return to camp. He was in no way depressed at his failure to find a way over the peak; there was still the alternative route to try Rather, he was enjoying the freedom and solace of his own company.

Somehow Larsen seemed to drain him, exhaust him mentally and physically, undermining his will-power, rendering him weak and indecisive. Alone he felt fitter, freer, more optimistic for the future, confident of his ability to survive. In Larsen he felt he had another burden to drag, in addition to the weight of the sledge, one which moved unwillingly, if at all. He sighed and then jerked himself to his feet. The air was growing chill, and it was still a long way to Anaktuvuk Pass. He arrived back at the camp in time to see Larsen hook and land his last fish.

14

The trout were a great success, more so than the caribou stew that followed. Their petrol stocks were diminishing fast. They had at most four days' supply remaining. Then, unless they could reach the lowlands and find more fuel, they would be forced to fall back on raw meat. As it was the stew was only half cooked, the meat flavourless and rubbery, the juices thin and unappetizing. Larsen found himself craving for salt. Any seasoning would be welcome, but salt was the flavour he missed most.

He had other cravings too. Though full fed, he felt dissatisfied, hungry, avid for the sort of food he could not have. For a time the popcorn had masked this desire, but now he longed for something sweet, chocolate cake or candy bars, yet paradoxically the thought made him feel queasy and sick. He longed too for starch, french fries and hamburgers, hash browns and cereals, especially bread. Endless visions of sandwiches passed through his mind, salami on rye, tuna fish, egg, corned beef, toasted cheese. Looking back, it seemed to him he'd lived on sandwiches all his life.

He remarked on this to Umiak, still mopping up the remains of the stew. Umiak laughed, but sympathetically, not sneering. 'Talk to my people and you will hear the same complaint, only the opposite way. After a spell eating what they call white man's food they too feel dissatisfied. They long for this, what they call "real food", and if they don't get it then after a while they feel weak and ill. They say it makes them "feel pale". Mind you, we acquired a craving for sweet things too, though we soon learned they were harmful. The coming of condensed milk and sugar brought an epidemic of tooth decay, among a people who had never known toothache in their lives.'

He fell silent, remembering the seal oil Larsen had so uselessly squandered. His mouth watered at the very thought of it, and a wave of anger and impatience swept over him. Then, realizing the futility of rancour, he pushed the recollection from his mind. Instead, he spoke of plans for the morning. 'The same as this afternoon, I thought. No sense both of us hauling the sledge up the mountain, only to have to turn back in the end. I can go faster than you, and it makes sense for you to rest that leg. How does it feel now?'

'Okay,' said Larsen casually. In fact it was aching badly, and he wondered if the jarring it had received earlier in the afternoon, while he was fishing, had aggravated it in any way. He decided though to say nothing, and to hope that a night's rest would mend the damage.

It was quite dark now, and under the clear skies the cold grew intense as the frost bit into the earth. The two men turned in, huddling together under their bedding. Larsen had lost any inhibitions he had at first felt about sharing a bed with Umiak. Warmth was paramount, and the bulkiness of their clothing rendered the experience devoid of any sense of intimacy. He felt weary, but the pain in his leg robbed him of sleep. Instead he lay watching the slow procession of the stars, trying not to think, trying not to move and disturb Umiak, who lay like a log at his side.

Suddenly Larsen was aware that the night was

growing lighter. The stars paled, snow drifts showed on the dark shoulder of the hill, and jagged rocks leaped into sharp relief. 'Can't be daylight already,' he murmured to himself.

'Moonlight,' said Umiak beside him. Larsen started with surprise. He had judged Umiak to be sound asleep.

'Moonlight,' repeated Umiak, 'somewhere behind the hill. I've been expecting it. In a day or so, if the weather holds, it will be nearly as light as day. Then we can travel all night if need be, and sleep during the day, when it's warmer.'

'For how long?' pondered Larsen. 'And how far?'

'I wish I knew,' said Umiak. 'But one thing's for sure, every mile takes us a little nearer, and with every day that passes the chance that we will meet up with a bunch of hunters increases. This time of year the people of Anaktuvuk hunt sheep in these hills. Or who knows, some rich trophy hunter may turn up in a helicopter.'

'We must be somewhere in the region that is going to be designated as the Gates of the Arctic National Park,' said Larsen.

'That's right. At least on the northern borders. But with twelve thousand square miles to wander round in, it's easy to get lost.'

Visions of Yellowstone National Park on a busy summer weekend, with harassed wardens trying to control queues of automobiles and camper wagons loaded with hot and frustrated tourists came to Larsen's mind. 'I can't see many people coming here for a vacation,' he grunted.

'They'll come,' answered Umiak shortly. 'In summer, when they can feed the bugs.'

A thought struck Larsen. 'There's no hunting allowed in national parks. How will your people get on?'

'Oh, they'll hunt, I guess, legally or illegally. As you may have noticed, it's a big place. It's going to be kinda hard to keep an eye on what folks are doing from day to day. Anyway, it's been promised that we will retain our traditional hunting rights as part of the land deal we worked out when the state chose their lands.'

Larsen recalled Umiak's remark to the pilot, on the morning of their fateful flight. 'If your government paid you compensation for land they had taken from you, you'd say it was nobody's goddamn business what you did with it.' At the time he had guessed Umiak was pretty touchy on the subject. Now he said, 'I guess you must feel pretty sore even so. No matter how good a deal you got, you still lost a lot of land you thought belonged to you.'

'We got a better deal than any other native American,' Umiak chuckled. 'But then, you see, we've never seen ourselves as land owners, rather as land users. Take this region, for instance. We've used it for ten thousand years or more, and yet it is as unchanged, as unspoilt, as it was the day we moved in. Which is more than you can say for most of the lower forty-eight.

'Now we maintained that seeing as how we'd been such good stewards in the past, we could be trusted to remain so in the future. We even offered to maintain the region as our own national park. It was a matter of pride, you see. Native pride, but it just wouldn't do. Maybe they thought we'd get robbed. Maybe, and a lot of people firmly believe this, they just didn't trust us.'

Instead, you have to trust us, thought Larsen. Privately, knowing the way some of the giant corporations operated, and the overall greed that prevailed, for mineral wealth in particular, he was not sure that such a trust might not be betrayed. Loyalty to his fellow whites kept him silent. All the same, he felt uneasy in his mind, recalling how often in the past few days he had mistrusted Umiak, only to discover that his own judgement had been hopelessly astray.

'Why should we trust you?' queried Umiak. 'Nothing personal, mind, but history records that it hasn't paid in the past. That is why I, among others, persuaded our people to register title to their land, even though they didn't regard it as theirs and so couldn't see the sense of it.'

He chuckled. 'I remember when the officials came to my home village to explain the policy of land registration. Everybody fell about laughing. One man said he was going to register a hilltop, because if too many people came up there they'd wear away the view. Another said he'd register a muskeg swamp, so if anyone walked on it he'd know Christ had returned, because Christ was the only guy he knew who could walk on water. My father was going to grow tomatoes.'

'Tomatoes!' exclaimed Larsen. 'Up here?'

'On a sandbank, up the river. It was a long-standing joke in the village. I'd been down south you see, and I brought lots of stuff back, including several pounds of fresh tomatoes, which no one in the village had ever seen. My father liked them, and he ate a lot, maybe too many, because he went off up the river and had to stop, urgently, on a big gravel bar in the middle of the stream.

'Later in the fall, he went up river again, hunting with a bunch of other guys. They stopped at the same bar to rest and eat, and there in the hollow where my father had squatted were tomato vines, growing everywhere, some with little fruit on them. They teased him plenty, I can tell you, told him he was a great shaman, asked him to eat gold dust and turn it into nuggets.'

Larsen laughed. 'What's a shaman?' he asked.

Umiak looked baffled, and faintly embarrassed. 'In the old religion, before the white missionaries came with their story of a Christ who died to save men from their sins, the shamans were our priests, our medicine men, spokesmen who could intercede on our behalf with the spirit world. They could heal the sick, or foretell the coming of the whales. They knew where the caribou were to be found. It is said that some could control the weather. It is certain that many had strange and terrible powers.'

'You believe in these powers?'

'The shamans are no more,' answered Umiak shortly. 'They have lost their power.' Suddenly he laughed again, at the memory of his father. 'I was telling you about the tomatoes. Point is, next year the sandbank had gone, washed away by the spring floods. That's how it is. A good fishing hole this year may yield nothing next. A berry patch might get burned over or eaten by bears, the caribou may winter in one spot for a while and then move on. So we use land, rather than own it. Still, we did register some land, and we were wiser than we knew, because a lot of that land lay in the way of the oil pipeline. To settle each individual claim would have taken years in the courts, so your people had to do a deal. Now at least we own nearly sixty thousand square miles. Not much out of half a million, but better than nothing. Plus we own the right to hunt and fish over federal lands, which, to be honest, is all many of my people ask.'

Larsen lay silent. A host of questions rose in his mind about this people who owned sixty thousand square miles they claimed they saw no sense in owning, who had millions of dollars in compensation money, who... But he was growing drowsy. The pain in his leg had eased now he had taken his weight off it, and he burrowed deeper into the thick hairs of the caribou pelt on which he lay. He had quickly grown accustomed to its rank animal odour. Now he almost welcomed it, associating it in his mind with rest and warmth and merciful sleep. It was strange, he thought sleepily, how quickly the mind grew to accept and even to find pleasure, in odours which were at first disagreeable, simply by their association with experiences that were pleasant.

Yet it seemed to him that now the smell was stronger, ranker, overlaid with the odour of decay. Was the hide, in spite of their care, beginning to decompose under the warmth of their bodies? Or was it Umiak? Was it his own unwashed body, or had the wound on his leg broken down again, turning gangrenous and necrotic under its dressing? The stench came again, in a warm foul wave, and he opened his eyes.

Larsen had met fear in many of its forms. He had felt the sudden paralysing fear that comes with near-death, and the following shock-wave of relief as it passed. He had endured its cold clammy grip as he waited for an unseen enemy to attack, lived with its stomach-scouring presence until his nerves seemed about to snap. He had fought the sudden panic that strikes for no reason when a man is alone in the night, and he had overcome it. Nothing in his experience had prepared him for the sight that now filled his gaze.

The bear stood not six feet away, and its bulk consumed the shadows of the night. He saw the small black eyes glittering in the starlight, the great teeth bared in an unholy grin. He smelled the foul carrion odour of its breath and saw the crusting of yellow ice and snow streaming down the broad chest like nicotine-stained saliva. Beyond, the bulk of the carcase, monstrous and bloated, blotted out the sky.

For a moment his throat constricted with terror. He actually felt the new bristles on his face erect. His heart began to thud, fast and preternaturally loud. Then his fear gave voice in an ear-splitting yell that was neither scream nor roar, but a great brassy trumpet blast of pent-up emotion and fury. Almost as if vaporized, the bear vanished.

Umiak shot bolt upright, still half asleep, gabbling incoherently. 'What the hell! Where? What is it?'

'The bear,' gasped Larsen, shaking now with the rigors of fear. 'That goddamned bear. It was right on top of us.'

Umiak sat and listened. The landscape lay deserted in

the pale blue-grey light. Nothing stirred. No sound broke the stillness of the Arctic night. 'There's nothing there. You were dreaming, maybe?'

Larsen snorted. 'This was no dream. The bastard was there. I saw him, smelled him, I could have damn near kicked him. He was as real and as solid as the Empire State building, and about as big. Man, I tell you, he was about to mash us into the ground.'

'Then where did he go?'

'Hell, I dunno,' grumbled Larsen. 'Guess I scared him off.'

'Not surprising,' said Umiak. 'You sure as hell scared me.'

Long minutes passed, both men listening, watching, then, 'There he is,' said Larsen.

Umiak stared long into the night, but nothing stirred. Nothing resembling a bear caught his eye. 'Where?' he asked, trying to keep the scepticism out of his voice.

'See that pillar-shaped rock across the river. He's there, watching us, the stinking son of a bitch.'

Umiak looked, but could see nothing. 'Don't look straight at the rock,' hissed Larsen. 'Shift your gaze a little to one side. You'll see him in the corner of your eye.'

Umiak did as he was bid. Suddenly the bear leaped into focus, a round snow-spattered bulk almost indistinguishable from the other boulders strewn across the landscape. Yet even as he watched he was aware that it moved, that it was slowly nodding its head.

'I got him.'

'What do you think?' asked Larsen.

'That's a good trick,' said Umiak.

'What is?'

'Seeing out of the corner of your eye. I never came across that one before. Where did you learn it?'

Jeez, thought Larsen. Anyone would think we were bird-watching. 'It was a dodge they taught us in the army. Something to do with the make-up of the eye.

They did explain, but I've forgotten. I only know it works. Came in handy on night patrol. What about the goddamned bear though?'

'I think he was hoping to find us dead, or at least catch us asleep. Most people I've heard of killed by bears have been dragged from their beds. Now he knows we're awake, he'll wait. As long as we're awake, and together, we're safe. I think.'

'You think,' repeated Larsen to himself. Slowly his fear was giving way to impotent rage. He found his fingers itching for the feel of an automatic rifle with which he could send down a hail of lead, reducing the bear to hamburger meat. Or better still, a burst of napalm. Instead he had to sit, powerless, weak, a prey not only to the bear but his own mounting fear. 'Why don't we scare him off?' he whispered.

'Because then we wouldn't know where he was,' explained Umiak. 'Do you really want to sit here, wondering all the while if he's crept round behind us?'

The thought did not appeal. 'Suppose he moves off, anyway?'

'Let's worry about that if it happens,' suggested Umiak.

Larsen's eyes began to prick and smart with the effort of keeping the bear in the periphery of his vision. Once he glanced away, only to feel a lurch of panic when he failed to locate the bear again straightaway. Slowly his hatred of the bear grew. What was he thinking of out there? What schemes were hatching in that evil, cunning brain?

Suddenly he realized he was being nonsensical. The bear was probably asleep. Logically there was no reason for it to attack unless they threatened it. Umiak seemed calm enough. Yet he knew the man had as much fear of the bear as he. He had just begun to relax when Umiak gripped his arm. 'He's on the move,' he whispered. Larsen looked towards the base of the rock, but the shape had gone. The bear had melted into the night.

Then the nightmare really began. As the moon waned, as the light fled from the hill and the darkness deepened the two men sat on, awake in the silence of the night. Try as he might, Larsen could not rid himself of the vision of the bear as it had appeared to him on opening his eyes. In his imagination he smelled again the rank putrescent odour of its breath. He felt the great jaws seize him, shake him, crush down into his skull.

Would it be quick? he wondered. Would he die from the first swift bone-crushing bite, or would the bear take him by the shoulder, the leg, the buttock, to drag him away, battering him over the ice-covered rocks? Again and again he felt his clothing ripped from his back by one stroke of those terrible claws, felt his ribs crack and the air whistle into the open cavity of his chest. He had seen too many men die slowly of wounds from which they could never recover. He had even shot one man, who steadfastly refused to die, or even to lose consciousness, although his head was half blown away and the lower part of his legless trunk was an unrecognizable bloody pulp. There was no one within a hundred miles who could perform the same service for him.

Then he remembered the knife, the one they had found in the cave. He knew just where it lay, in the canteen, no more than a yard from his hand. If the bear came, he could use it, if not on the bear, at least on himself. At least he would die swiftly.

Beside him he felt Umiak stir, and a lurch of fear rocked him as he wondered what the man had seen or heard. Then Umiak's voice reassured him. 'I've had an idea for a kind of bear deterrent, should he show up again.'

Carefully he explained his plan. 'We still have the remains of the pilot's pants, and we've got about ten feet of fine cable spare that we took from the plane. If we fasten a lump of rag to the end of the wire, and decant a drop of gasolene into the cup from the vacuum flask, we'll have the makings of a flaming torch we can whirl around our heads if we're attacked. You stay ready with the lighter, I'll stand by with the gas, and if our buddy shows up again we'll singe his eyebrows. It'll be a brave bear that will face up to that.'

Larsen laughed with glee, striving, not altogether successfully, to keep the rising hysteria out of his voice. Together they worked in the dark, and when all was ready they sat back again. Then long hours passed, and they waited, Larsen half hoping the bear would show up again. But the bear never came. Shaking with cold and fatigue the two men watched the dawn break, and saw blessed light steal over the valley, flooding the deserted landscape.

15

With morning came renewed courage. Umiak insisted on carrying on with his plan to explore the second valley, leaving Larsen in camp to rest and pack their belongings in readiness to move off, in either direction. Larsen would have preferred to accompany him, not wishing to be left alone in the solitude of the mountains, but pride prevented him from making more than a token protest. If Umiak was prepared to face the wilderness alone and unarmed, in the certain knowledge that a hungry and dangerous bear lurked somewhere close by, then he too could endure the same ordeal. It would not be long, a couple of hours at most, and then they would be on the move once more, though in which direction he did not dare to speculate.

He watched Umiak depart, and then sank back on a rock. There was no hurry. Their few belongings could be stowed and lashed on the sledge in a few minutes. Meantime it would do no harm to let the bedding air. He spread it out, turning the caribou hide hair side down, and then turned his attention to a chore he had been dreading, an inspection of the wound on his leg.

The wound itself looked clean, and what little discharge there was looked clear, without any trace of odour or suppuration. It was the size of it that appalled him. The original incision, where Umiak had lanced the abscess, had now widened and grown so distorted that no trace of the cut remained. Instead there was an irregularly shaped ulcerated hole, a pit of naked flesh, around which the skin curled back, and from which crimson florets of blood blossomed as he peeled off the dressing.

He felt totally at a loss as to how to treat it. At first he thought it might benefit from exposure to the air but the cold affected it immediately, and even the light breeze caressing the naked flesh caused him such intense pain that he was glad to cover it again with what remained of the shirt he had sacrificed as a dressing. Padded and protected from the cold, it felt easier, and he resolved then not to touch it again if he could avoid it.

All the same, prudence made him wash the soiled dressing in the stream and spread it out on the rocks to dry. He had just completed this task and was striving to restore some warmth to his frozen fingers, when he caught a glimpse of a streak of white racing across the side of the hill. As he watched it appeared again, an arctic fox fleeing from some unseen threat. Once it checked, to turn and stare down the valley, before vanishing once more from view.

Larsen wondered what could have disturbed it. Certainly not Umiak, for he had gone off in the opposite direction. With a sense of growing unease, Larsen walked to the foot of the pool. Then, seeing nothing, he climbed up on to the rock that overhung the gorge.

Then he saw it, far away downstream, but moving in his direction, the shaggy bulk of the bear that had haunted them since they had left the plane. Surprisingly he felt quite calm, detached, able to watch with interest as the bear picked its way slowly upstream. It seemed in no hurry, pausing from time to time to look from side to side, or just standing, swinging its great head, before moving on with a fluid, effortless grace. So Larsen wasted precious minutes, hoping the bear would turn aside, or change its mind and head off back downstream.

Suddenly it dawned on him that the bear had no such intention. As the full danger of the situation came to him his mind began to race. His heart hammered and his mouth went dry. He felt his knees begin to tremble violently so that he sank down on the rock, desperately trying to think clearly and logically. Would he be safe up here on the rock? Would the bear pass by without scenting his presence? If so, he would have to watch helplessly as the bear demolished what was left of their food supplies? Worse, it might move on and pull down Umiak, somewhere alone up there among the crags. On the other hand, if the bear got wind of his presence, he was dead.

Then a cold rage and a hatred of the bear overwhelmed his fear. Above all, he longed to destroy it, to rid himself of its menace for ever. As on the previous night he longed for a weapon, a fragmentation grenade, napalm, any of the tools of war with which he had in the past confronted the enemy.

To reach the camp the bear had to pass below him, unless it crossed the stream. It had no reason to do that. If only he had a rock heavy enough to drop on it, but there was nothing to hand bigger than his closed fist. Still, he had time to scramble down off the rock and climb back with one big enough, if he could manage it. If not, Umiak's torch might scare it away.

Only he didn't want just to scare it away. He wanted to annihilate it for ever, to be free of it so that he could sleep at nights. It came to him then what he must do, and there was little time left if he was to put his plan into action. He took one last glance down the valley. Unless the bear increased its pace, he had several more minutes at least.

With extreme care he climbed down off the rock. To slip now would be fatal. With his knife he cut about a foot of cable from Umiak's torch, and tore a small strip of rag from the bundle. His hands, he noticed, worked without a tremor. Then he fastened the rag to one end of the cable, and took one of the plastic bags, a whole day's supply of fuel, and fastened the other end round its neck. First though, he soaked the rag fuse in petrol, not too much, for he didn't want flaming petrol dripping on to the bag while he held it in his hands, and not too little, lest the spirit evaporate before the time came to light the fuse. Then he climbed back up on to the rock, thankful that Umiak had left the lighter with him.

The bear was still some distance away, so he had time to spare. To his dismay he found he was shaking so violently he was afraid that when the time came he would be unable to work the lighter, or even fumble and let it slip from his grasp. It took all his will-power to calm himself, to clench and unclench his fists, to breathe deeply and slowly and so relax. Meanwhile the bear came on. Now he could see its breath steaming in the cold air, and Larsen found himself marvelling at the coating of snow and ice that crusted its hair and hung matted and stained to its flanks. Yet it had a strange beauty, an aura of grace and power, seeming so gentle and harmless that even now Larsen found it hard to believe that the bear posed any sort of a threat.

Now the bear had almost reached the rock. A few seconds more and it would be directly below him. Larsen's thumb poised over the wheel of the lighter, his plastic fire-bomb firmly gripped in his left hand. Sudden panic seized him. How long would the bomb take to drop? Should he change his grip, hold the bag in his right hand instead of his left? Would the lighter work first time?

Even as he was thinking the bear passed beneath him. Remote, detached, he watched his right hand light the fuse, saw the plastic bag curve outwards and downwards, a shining silver ball followed by a tiny tag of crimson and yellow. It burst square on the bear's head, dissolving into a shower of sparkling drops that exploded round the bear and dissolved into nothing.

For a long time nothing happened. The bear stopped dead in its tracks, began to rear up on its hind legs, and then, like a great flower blossoming, exploded into flame. Larsen gazed transfixed, horrified, at the spectacle below him. Liquid flame dripped from the bear's jowels. Its ears flamed like torches and its massive paws burst into pillars of fire that ran down its arms as it beat at its head. For an instant Larsen saw little rivulets of flame playing round its eyes, then a pall of steam and smoke clouded his vision and a stench of singed hair reached his nostrils.

Dimly Larsen was aware of agonized bellowing, of himself screaming and cursing, and then, as suddenly as it had begun, the fire went out. The bear was down, rolling and writhing in agony, half in and half out of the stream. Then it was still, and Larsen heaved a long shuddering sigh of relief. As he gazed down at the motionless hulk below him he felt a wave of elation and savage joy.

Only the bear was not dead. Even as Larsen began to taste the sweet savour of revenge the great beast stirred, rose drunkenly to its feet, and then, to Larsen's unspeakable horror, it began to dance. It reared up on its hind legs, took a few tottering steps, fell on all fours and then rose again, unable to endure the pain of its burned pads on the cold ground. It swung its head wildly from side to side, stepped forward and back, gyrating round as the Arctic wind tormented the scorched flesh of its face. Centuries before, itinerant bear trainers had taught their charges to dance in just such a manner, walking them over hot coals to the beating of a drum. Now a similar drum beat accompanied the macabre dancing of the bear, but it was only the thudding of Larsen's heart.

Sightless eyes stared out at Larsen, seeming to sense his presence even though they could not see. The bear staggered towards him, its jaw chattering with mingled pain and rage, saliva drooling in long shining strands from the raw rim of its burned and blackened jaws. Unbelievably, it began to climb the rock, hauling itself upwards over the jagged stones, two feet, a yard, six feet, drawing itself ever nearer, and all the time a rasping bubbling moan accompanied the slow scrabble of its claws on the frozen rock. Larsen closed his eyes. He could watch no more.

A dull thud below him told him the bear had fallen. Scarce daring to look he crawled to the edge and peered over, in time to see the bear lurching and staggering away among the rocks. In a moment it was gone, Larsen knew not where. For a wild moment he considered following it, to finish the task he had begun, although how he was not exactly sure. Already he was beginning to realize the futility of pursuit. He might search for a week and never find the bear again. With a sickening sense of dread he became aware that he could not be sure that he had rid himself of the menace of the bear. It could still return. Wearily he climbed down off the rock and began packing their gear.

Umiak returned to find him sitting by the stream, staring out across the valley. 'All well?' he queried.

'The bear came back,' replied Larsen dully.

There was a pause while Umiak digested this. 'What happened?'

Larsen told him, starting with his sight of the fleeing fox. Umiak listened without interruption, and then let out a long low whistle of amazement. 'You're crazy, man. You know that? Crazy!'

Larsen nodded. 'It seemed a good idea at the time.'

Umiak shrugged. 'That's the story of mankind, I guess. Well, that bear is wolf bait from now on. Once they find him, and that won't take long, and realize he's blind and helpless, they won't rest until they've pulled him down. Good thing in a way. It'll keep them from pestering us.'

Suddenly Larsen felt better. The thought that the wolves would finish his work had not occurred to him. 'Sorry about the waste of gas.'

'So you traded a hot meal for a night's sleep. Not such a bad deal after all. Besides, we could sleep by a fire tonight. The pass is clear, and the way ahead is downhill for miles. Come on. Let's see how far we can get.'

All at once he began to laugh. 'Of all the crazy stunts. Roasting a bear alive. Beats just about anything I ever heard. I just wish I'd been there to see it.'

Larsen said nothing. Somehow he could not rid himself of the fear that the bear would return. It had begun to seem indestructible. Sooner or later it would revive, recover sufficiently once more to pick up the trail, to follow them until it had exacted the vengeance it was due. Besides, Umiak's callous humour and indifference to the bear's ultimate fate sickened and disgusted him. He had not meant it to happen like that. The bear should have died so that he could have shown the corpse to Umiak and triumphed over the kill. Later they could have dined on bear steaks and so justified the kill. Without a word he took hold of the towline of the sledge. He did not look back. He feared what he might see.

16

Now the way led steadily downhill. The going was good on the firm wind-packed snow, and on either side the mountains receded away into the distance as with every mile the valley broadened out into a wide sunlit plain. In the distance a river gleamed, a river whose waters flowed due east. Unless it took a dramatic turn to the north or south, Umiak was sure that ultimately it would lead them to safety.

All the same he was uneasy in his mind. Deeply engrained on his psyche was the age-old belief among his people that to cause unnecessary harm or suffering to an animal was to bring bad luck. As a boy an old shaman had spoken to him of the Keepers of the Game, the spirits that watched over every animal in their care, that tolerated hunting because man had to kill to live, but who would be sure to avenge any abuse of an animal, living or dead. Few hunters now gave a dead seal a drink of water so that it would not be thirsty on its journey to the spirit world, but men still blamed their lack of success in hunting on some infringement of the ancient code, such as wasting food, or failing to dispose of the remains in a proper manner.

Now he felt guilty, remembering his own exultation at the fate of the bear. Maybe Larsen had brought them bad luck, misfortune he would have to share. There were no shamans left now. One by one they had lost their power and died. Even if there were, there wasn't one near to intercede on their behalf. He thought of praying to the white man's god, about whom he had been taught at school. Yet such a being seemed so remote as to be inaccessible. His mother had taught him that the Christian faith was a good working religion. 'But,' she added, 'sometimes we need something a bit special. Someone who understands our ways and needs.'

There was no way in which he could explain his fears and doubts to Larsen. In any case the man had suffered enough. He trudged at his side, silent, uncommunicative, uncomplaining, yet his eyes were those of a dead man. Somehow Umiak sensed that this was more than the aftermath of fear, rather a mental trauma that went far deeper.

The long hours passed. Slowly the distant stream drew nearer. The sun, low on the horizon, paused briefly on Umiak's right shoulder, and their shadows walked beside them in the snow, seeming to outdistance them as they grew longer. Umiak's legs ached with every step, his feet were frozen beyond feeling, leaden useless lumps that grew heavier with every stride and threatened to cramp his muscles into agonizing knots. Beside him Larsen walked as if in a dream, stumbling from time to time but always regaining his balance without falling completely.

Willow thickets bordered the stream. Willow or poplar, Umiak could not make out which, and when he tried to focus his gaze the vista swam before his eyes. Either way, the vegetation promised both shelter and fire, if they could get there in time. The ground sloped less now and the surface had become more uneven, a series of gentle humps and rises. The sledge grew heavier, their pace slower, yet Umiak knew that were he to stop moving, even for an instant, his will would be unequal to the effort of further movement. Anxiously he glanced at Larsen. The man seemed to be sleepwalking, his head held high, his gaze directed upwards. Each faltering step he took jarred the towline of the sledge and threatened to pitch them headlong in the snow. Umiak bent his shoulder in an effort to take more of the weight of the sledge, and plodded on.

So they reached the river, and a snow-covered gravel bar on the edge of a dense willow thicket. The leaves of the willows were gone now but the stems grew tall and densely packed, offering shelter from the wind. Wearily Umiak cut a bundle of twigs and began to sweep a space clear of snow. He looked to Larsen for help, but the man was sitting on the sledge, staring stonily down the stream, and making no move to unpack the bedding. So it was Umiak who cut willow boughs to spread on the ground and laid the caribou skin over them. He took Larsen by the arm and led him unprotesting to the bed, covered him with rugs, and turned to gather firewood.

When he returned Larsen was fast asleep. Umiak began to make a fire, but found he was physically incapable of the effort. His fingers refused to obey the demands of his brain. Waves of darkness swept across his vision, his arms felt leaden and useless, and twice he felt himself pitching forward, jerking himself upright just in time to prevent himself sprawling headlong on the gravel. At last he abandoned his attempts. He just had strength to crawl in beside Larsen before he lost consciousness. His last thought, before he fell asleep, was that they ought to eat.

He woke to bright moonlight and intense cold. Beside him Larsen jerked and moaned in his sleep. It must have been this that aroused him. For a time he lay still, trying to get back to sleep again, but hunger pains and a growing chill kept him awake. The night was well spent and the moon rode high in the sky, shedding its brilliant light over the snow-covered landscape, and Umiak noted with quiet satisfaction that the makings of a fire lay neatly sorted at his feet. He had only the dimmest recollection of putting them there, but it would take no more than a few moments to start a blaze.

Carefully, so as not to disturb Larsen, he crept out from under the bedding, feeling the muscles of his legs and back shriek in protest as he did so. Then he laid the tinder at his feet and began to pile thin twigs in pyramid fashion round it. As the grass caught into flame he added larger twigs, and then the thickest branches he had been able to find.

Soon the warmth of the blaze began to make itself felt on his face and hands. He set the sledge on its side to reflect more of the warmth, brought water from the stream in the canteen and set a stew on the flames to cook. Meanwhile he sat luxuriating in the warmth, allaying the worst of his hunger by chewing a slab of dried meat. Their food supplies were running low already, but food gave energy, strength to combat the cold as well as fuel the muscles of their bodies. Once Larsen cried out in his sleep, but still did not wake. It occurred to Umiak that the man might sleep more peacefully if he had some food inside him, so as soon as the stew was ready he leaned across the fire and shook Larsen by the foot.

Larsen came awake with a jerk. He opened his eyes and saw a world lurid with flames, from the centre of which a black bulk loomed out over him. Dark eyes reflected fire, and white teeth bared in a grin. He gave one gasp of fear and flung aside the bedding. Next moment he was running, fleeing for his life up the valley, stumbling, falling, picking himself up and floundering on, desperate in his attempt to escape the bear that had haunted him in his dreams and had now returned to destroy him.

Stunned, astonished, Umiak watched him go. Then he called, 'Larsen, Larsen, come back. Larsen, it is Umiak.'

At last, to his intense relief, he saw Larsen slow down,

stop, and then turn and walk slowly back. Umiak did not move from his place by the fire, but his hand sought the knife that lay close by. If Larsen's mind had snapped, he could be dangerous. Carefully he hid the knife where Larsen could not see it but where he could reach it again in a hurry, if need be.

Larsen, however, was sheepish and contrite, but otherwise sane again. 'I thought you were that goddamned bear come to get me again.'

Umiak said nothing, simply offering Larsen a cup of steaming stew. Larsen took it gratefully and sank down beside the fire, still panting from his exertions.

'All day I've been seeing nothing else but the bear with its head on fire. All night I've dreamed about it, and then when you woke me, leaning over the fire... ' He shuddered, and drank the hot stew.

For a while Umiak said nothing. Then, when he spoke, it was with a quiet assurance he did not entirely feel. 'The bear is dead by now, it will follow us no more. You did what you had to, the only way you could. The way ahead now is clear, so you must eat and sleep, and save your strength. No more midnight races in the snow.'

Larsen nodded. Soon, warmed by the fire and the hot food, they slept again, and this time Larsen's sleep was deep and dreamless. Both men woke cheerful and refreshed, and once more ravenously hungry. The moment he put his weight on his injured leg, however, he knew he was in trouble. The pain was so intense he had to bite his lip to keep from shouting out loud. His midnight flight, he reflected ruefully, had not done it any good at all.

Umiak was some distance away, collecting dead willow branches for the fire. Larsen hitched up his trouser leg and took a look. The dressing was soaked and oozing blood and puss. Hearing Umiak return, Larsen hid the dressing from sight again. His shame and humiliation over his behaviour earlier were hard enough to bear. He did not want Umiak to find out that he might jeopardize them still further. Whatever the damage was, he could do nothing about it and to interfere with the bandage might make matters worse. At all costs, he must keep going, crawl if necessary, for with their food supplies all but exhausted they had to reach safety or starve...

The bear lay by the ice-fringed waters of a stream, his paws chilled and soothed by the flow of the current, his great jaws hanging just below the surface of the water. So he found some comfort and relief, and from time to time he was able to swallow and so assuage his raging thirst. Some sight had returned to one eye, so he knew it was dawn, but the surrounding rocks were but grey blurs veiled by a curtain of light.

He still felt the power of life within him, and during the long night that had passed he had discovered that as long as he supported most of his weight on his hind legs, and curled his forepaws inwards so that only the backs touched the earth, he could progress tolerably well. His hearing remained acute, and for the moment he was content to rest, and even doze a little, as he let the stream do its healing work. Above him a raven swung in great lazy circles in the sky. The raven knew that the behaviour of the bear was unnatural, and that in itself was worthy of note. All the same, the time of the killing was not yet near, and with a tilt of its wing the raven rode the wind until it vanished into the tundra.

The long day passed, and presently the bear rose and moved slowly downstream to where the waters pitched over a shelf of rock to fall fifty feet on to a steeply sloping bed of scree. Some of the waters were lost, blown away as spume that vaporized into thin air. The remainder vanished from sight, soaking into loose porous shale that lay below. The bear paused, hesitating on the brink, instinctively sensing the void below. Then he turned away to seek the shelter of a sun-warmed rock. There he slept again, moaning softly from time to time as the flickering fires of pain played again around his jaws.

The wolf pack came with the setting of the sun. Instantly the bear awoke, his nostrils filled with the strong feral scent of their presence, even though he could not discern their shapes. With his back to the rock he growled a warning, even though he was sure they would not attack. The wolves might have left him then, sensing he had no kill to guard, no meat that they might steal. Yet within moments of their arrival they knew there was something wrong with the bear.

The power of speech is a gift for which a price has been paid. So over the millennia mankind has become blind and deaf and insensitive to a thousand clues and signs to which the rest of the natural world is ever alert. A wolf pack might appraise a herd of fifty caribou and know at once which individual is slightly lame, which is weakened by an infestation of parasites, which is feeling the infirmity of increasing age. For ten years or more a big bull may easily outrun and outdistance a wolf pack, may even be so confident of his strength and power that he does not even trouble to flee. The wolves know this. They also know that there will come a day when the bull can no longer run, and they will wait patiently for this day. Left alone the bull might survive another decade. Once he has betrayed his weakness his life is numbered in days.

Now, all unwittingly, the bear too had betrayed his plight, and the wolves grew bold. Tentatively the lead wolf ran in and snapped at a hind paw, instantly leaping clear lest a scything sweep of a forepaw flay him alive. No such retaliation came. Others now risked attack, unable to inflict any harm against the matted frozen pelt of the bear, but enraging him, unsettling him, bolting him from his scanctuary beside the rock.

Now he whirled in blind fury, lashing out at his unseen attackers as they came from all sides. He could hear them and smell them, but he could not see them, and time and time again his claws cut the empty air, inches away from the leaping muscular bodies of the excited wolves. Above the angry roars of the tormented bear came a chorus of snarls, a frenzied barking, and even a high-pitched yapping from one of the younger wolves. The lead wolf though attacked in silence.

Now the bites were beginning to tell, a dozen slashes from curved white fangs on the thinner skin of the bear's hocks and forearms, so that blood flew in a fine spray as the bear struck out right and left. This was the wolves' way, for a wolf cannot kill outright. Rather it aims to cripple and maim, to weary its victim and weaken it from loss of blood. Meanwhile, slowly but surely, the pack was unwittingly driving the bear to the edge of the nearby cliff.

On the very brink the lead wolf made an error of judgement. He caught the bear on the snout and held on a fraction of a second too long. As he released his hold he felt the bear crush his foreleg between his jaws, and as he struggled to be free he felt the bear back away, tormented by the others who, taking advantage of the situation, had flung themselves on his hindquarters.

The ground at the edge of the cliff was soft with the action of the stream. For untold centuries it had been crumbling away, broken by the bite of the frost and dried to powder by the summer sun and wind. Suddenly the earth began to move, and with one accord the wolves leaped clear, all save the one imprisoned in the bear's jaws. Bear and wolf and hundreds of tons of earth and rock and silt slid over the precipice to crash down on to the scree below. The wolf was flung away, to die instantly under a hailstorm of falling rocks.

For a moment the bear lived on, but as the first booming crash of the rock fall echoed and died among the hills, there came a deeper, more ominous rumble. A giant rock, poised since the Ice Age on the edge of the cliff above, now loosed its last precarious hold. Slowly it slid down the scree. Almost gently it pinned the old bear down among the rocks, pushing him with inexorable force into the yielding earth, driving the breath from his lungs and binding his chest tight so he was unable to breathe. For a minute or so the bear fought with all his strength, and then darkness filled his mind. His heart slowed, weakened, fluttered awhile, and then was still.

Each step was agony for Larsen, as if his leg pumped liquid fire with every stride. Try as he might he could not help limping, and soon, despite the cold, he could feel sweat breaking out on his brow. He felt sick and faint, but somehow he kept going, and though Umiak must have noticed, he said nothing.

They forged their way steadily down the valley, following the stream but occasionally having to make wide detours in order to skirt willow thickets so dense as to make the way impassable. On either side the hills rose silent and deserted. No tracks showed in the snow, no raven flew overhead. The two men were no more than tiny dots in the vast white silent landscape. Ahead they could see mountains again. Umiak prayed that somehow the stream would lead them through or round them.

Time passed, the valley grew perceptibly narrower, the way downhill steeper. Now the stream was racing beside them, as if it too was anxious to escape the winter and the bonds of ice which would hold it fast until spring. Then they stopped, staring in dismay at the prospect before them. Ahead the stream forked before entering yet another river, one which once more flowed to the north. Before them, on the far side of the valley, the mountains rose like a wall.

'I don't believe it,' said Larsen. 'I just don't believe it. We might be going round in circles.' But Umiak wasn't listening. Instead he was staring intently up the valley.

'Look.' He pointed and Larsen stared in the direction of his outstretched arm. Tiny black dots littered the frozen plain, and as he watched one after another jerked skywards as though pulled by strings, only to float back down to earth.

'Ravens,' he said dully. 'What of it?'

'So many,' said Umiak softly. 'There must be a hundred or more. Only a great killing would attract that number.' Suddenly he grabbed Larsen by the arm. 'Don't you see?' he asked excitedly. 'Don't you understand? There must have been a caribou hunt here just recently. That means my people cannot be far away. Come on.'

He set off up the valley, scarcely waiting for Larsen to catch up. As they neared the site the ravens rose in a black cloud, and across the river they could see the broad trail where the caribou had trekked southward through the snow, bloodstained patches where deer had died, and fragments of entrail strewn like garish ribbons over the valley floor. But Umiak paid little heed to these. Instead he pointed to twin tracks leading away like railway lines away upstream. 'Snowmobile tracks,' he shouted. 'If we can just find a way across the river, we can follow them.'

Larsen felt a pang of dismay. The river looked dangerously fast and deep, its leaden waters swirling over hidden rocks and foaming down into deep forbidding pools. In spite of their predicament he could not help but wish, given more fortunate circumstances, he could cast a line over some of the more inviting stretches. Now he wondered if he'd ever survive to fish again. 'It's no good,' he stammered. 'I can't cross. I can't wade. Look.'

Umiak sucked his teeth in dismay at the sight of Larsen's dressing. Then he shrugged, and turning away began exploring upstream. After a while he beckoned to Larsen to follow. Larsen did so, dragging the sledge behind him. Already Umiak was pulling off his sealskin boots. 'Give me my old boots out of the holdall,' he ordered.

Larsen did so and Umiak put them on. 'Should keep the cold out for a while,' he commented. 'Right then, climb on my back.'

'Hey, just a minute,' protested Larsen.

'Climb on!' yelled Umiak. 'Or stay there. It's your choice.'

'No. Listen a minute,' insisted Larsen. 'We still have the freezer bags, half a dozen big ones, and some sealing tape. We can wade across dry-shod.'

Umiak's face lit up. 'Good job someone in this outfit's got some brains.'

He had chosen a wide shallow at which to cross, and bearing the sledge between them they set off, feeling their way cautiously over the river-bed. Nowhere was the water more than knee deep but the current was so strong that with every step it threatened to sweep them off their feet. Twice Larsen stumbled and almost fell, but each time he managed to right himself, and still keep a grip on the sledge.

At last they reached the opposite bank where Umiak changed back into his sealskin boots with a sigh of relief. No water had penetrated their makeshift waders but Larsen's feet were numb with cold. He longed to stamp about to restore the circulation but did not dare. At least the cold had anaesthetized the pain somewhat.

Umiak shook his head sorrowfully over the snow-mobile tracks. 'Two days, maybe three days old,' he estimated. 'The hunters will be far away by now. Pity they only killed as many deer as they could carry. If they'd cached a few, we could simply have waited here until they returned.'

Once more the trail led uphill, but with a trail to follow they were confident they could not wander astray again, even though the tracks led south. By late afternoon they reached the lake.

17

'I know where I am,' said Umiak.

Larsen looked out over the frozen surface of the lake, rose-pink in the light of the setting sun, then back at the burnt-out remains of the camp-fire, the trampled snow, and the rectangle that marked the site of a tent. 'Your friends must have camped here.'

Umiak nodded. 'Last night maybe. It's a regular spot. I camped here myself, oh, many years ago.'

'How far?' queried Larsen.

'To Anaktuvuk?' Umiak smiled brightly. 'Oh, not far now.'

'Look,' said Larsen. 'I may be a stranger round here, but I'm not dumb. Your people stayed over for the night here. Now if they'd been on their doorstep, they would have kept going, especially with a snowmobile. So how far? Fifty, a hundred miles?'

Umiak looked shocked. 'No, no, not as far as that. Forty miles perhaps.'

Larsen felt better, but not much. Forty miles, on a leg that was threatening to give up at any moment, when every step was an effort, was still a long way. All the same, he would make it, even if he had to crawl.

They made themselves as comfortable as possible. The brush was thicker here. Alder and willow, mingled with poplar and scrub birch, grew in dense thickets, and on the slope of the hills berry bushes showed dark against the snow. Even though they had the comfort of a fire and enough food to satisfy their hunger, Larsen could not help contrasting their lot with that of the hunting party. He had visions of the tent, bright with light and cosy with the warmth of a kerosene stove. A down sleeping bag, coffee, sweet and hot, and thick caribou steaks fried in their own fat.

Umiak must have been sharing his thoughts. 'Pity we didn't get here earlier,' he remarked. 'Some company would have been nice.'

'Tired of mine then?' asked Larsen.

Umiak was immediately embarrassed. 'Oh no, Mr Larsen,' he stammered. 'I didn't mean...'

Larsen laughed. 'That's okay. I know exactly what you meant. In any case, as you said yourself, man is a social animal.' Umiak's formal mode of address suddenly struck him as utterly incongruous. 'Tell me, what have your people got against the use of Christian names?' It occurred to him then that Umiak might not have been baptized. 'Or should I say first name?'

It was Umiak's turn to laugh. 'Oh, I was christened, by a Presbyterian minister, and at school I was taught it was the only true faith, and that the beliefs of my forefathers were just stupid superstition. Later on, at high school –'

'You went to high school?' Larsen interjected.

'Sure,' said Umiak impatiently. 'In Kansas. Lots of us did.'

'You liked it there?'

'No. I was glad to get back home. All the same, I learned a lot. I learned that there were other "true" religions, like Buddhism and Hinduism, and found there was truth in all of them, including the old beliefs of my own people.'

'But that still doesn't explain why you don't like using first names,' persisted Larsen.

Umiak hesitated. 'Now that is perhaps a foolishness. A

silly superstition if you like, but there is an old belief that if you tell another person your given name, you put yourself in his power.'

Larsen was about to scoff. Then he remembered. He had told Umiak his name, and virtually all along he had been at the man's mercy. It was an uneasy feeling on which to sleep. For a while he lay wakeful, excited at the thought that at last their ordeal was almost at an end, yet afraid that at the last moment something might go wrong. How long? he wondered, before their journey's end. Forty miles did not sound far. If the going was good, another two days should see them to safety. He reckoned they must have covered twenty miles at least that very day, even though the last hours had been torture. Now, as he rested, the pain in his leg was subsiding. Tomorrow morning it would be as stiff and sore as hell, but usable, he fervently hoped.

They broke camp soon after daylight. Umiak seemed unusually preoccupied and withdrawn, busying himself lashing down the bedding on the sledge as Larsen tested his leg, gritting his teeth against the pain and willing it to work, hoping the torment would ease. There was a haziness about the light, and he thought he detected a faint warmth in the breeze that blew from the east, or maybe it was that he was simply growing acclimatized to the cold.

They set off, Umiak setting a deliberately slow pace, following the last river along what they hoped would be the last valley they would traverse. On either side the mountains towered two thousand feet above them. The valley widened out and they passed another, smaller, lake. Here the stream ended, but a little further on they topped a small rise to find another flowing away downhill.

At any other time Larsen would have been impressed by the scenery as it unfolded. Now he was deaf and blind to his surroundings, willing himself forward, heedless of the breeze that blew cold on his face and stung his eyes, conscious only of the need to keep walking, to choose where he set his left foot down, to lean heavily on his right foot, step after step after step. So he failed to notice that the sun had vanished in the haze, that the mountain peaks, earlier distant and seemingly shrunken against the sky, now loomed nearer, as though threatening to hem them in. A grunt from Umiak brought him back to reality. 'What's up?' he queried.

Umiak nodded towards the east. 'Storm coming,' he announced. 'Big one. I think our luck just ran out.'

Larsen stared into the distance. The sky overhead was grey but the horizon was obscured by a violet veil of cloud. Even as he watched it seemed to grow. Ragged pinnacles smoked and fumed from its upper layers, to be snatched away and torn to dark shreds by some unseen force. Its underside bulged ominously and a flicker of lightning played briefly on its flank. 'I guess we ought to take cover,' he muttered.

'And fast,' said Umiak. 'But where?'

To the north the southward-facing flank of the hill was shaggy with scrubby brush, stunted by the cold but offering thicker cover than the northern-facing slopes. Yet here the valley was over a mile wide, and to reach the scrub they would have to cross the stream. Rocks and boulders, the litter of centuries of erosion, lay to their right, and it was towards these that the two men headed. Try as he might Larsen could not move faster than a slow walk. Umiak took the sledge from him and raced ahead, pounding uphill as fast as his labouring lungs would allow. By the time Larsen reached him he had found a small niche in the rocks, unloaded the sledge, and was wedging it on its side as a windbreak.

Feverishly he piled rocks against the base, anchoring it as best he could against the storm-force winds that were already howling around them, his breath coming in great laboured gasps as he struggled with the stones.

Larsen bent to help him, but Umiak waved him away. 'Spread the bedding,' he shouted, 'and lie on it, for God's sake. Don't let it blow away. Any minute now we won't be able to stand.'

As if to prove the truth of his forecast, the first gust slammed against them with solid force. Larsen staggered back, and then flung himself forward on to the pile of bedding. As he dragged it into the lee of the sledge he saw Umiak fly past, thrown off his feet and sent sprawling in the snow. Umiak made no further attempt to stand up, but crawled slowly back, hugging the earth. Between them they unrolled the bedding and crawled into it, rolling it round them so that their own weight held it down. Umiak had already stowed the rest of their gear among the rocks. They could only hope it would stay secure.

Another violent gust swept the valley. The sledge trembled and shook against their backs, but it held firm, and they cowered against it as lightning split the sky and the thunder echoed and re-echoed between the hills. Snow began to fly past, driven horizontally by the wind, swirling in great white sheets over the frozen terrain, eddying round them, flicking like frozen darts against their faces, so that they buried their heads against the sting. Larsen lay next to the sledge, Umiak beside him, shaking with cold and exertion, his breath coming in great rasping sobs which seemed never to get less, so that on impulse Larsen put his arms around him and drew him tight to his body, striving to share what little warmth he possessed. It seemed to work, and slowly Umiak relaxed, his breathing eased, and by and by Larsen thought he slept.

Outside the darkness deepened until it seemed that night had come before its time. At intervals lightning lit the scene, and Larsen watched the driving snow, felt the sledge hammering against his spine, waited for the thunder, and expected any moment that the storm would rip their frail shelter away, seize them and smash them in its iron fist. So the long seconds ticked by, hour after hour, while the wind howled and screamed as it drove among the rocks. Gradually, his senses numbed by the din, Larsen fell into a half coma, half doze, from which he surfaced from time to time only to hear the fury of the storm still raging about them.

When next he woke it was with a sense of suffocation. Pushing the bedding back off his face, he discovered they were buried deep in snow, soft and powdery and frozen. It was still dark, but the clamour of the storm had ceased, the air was still, and above him stars shone in the sky. Exhausted, he drifted back to slumber again, this time a deep dreamless sleep, while beside him Umiak lay cold and still.

Day broke, and with the light Larsen struggled to regain consciousness. A new sound disturbed the silence, a soft rasping that at first Larsen was unable to identify. Then, as the clouds of sleep cleared from his mind, he realized it was Umiak's breathing, shallow, fast and unnaturally loud. The man appeared to be sleeping, but his face was flushed, and small beads of perspiration had formed on his forehead.

He was not asleep, though, and he opened his eyes as he felt Larsen's stare, trying to smile as he saw the other man's concern.

'I'm in trouble this time,' he whispered.

Larsen nodded. 'Looks like you're starting pneumonia.'

'Feels like it. Hurts when I breathe.' Umiak closed his eyes again. 'Serves me right. Too much exertion, getting overheated and then chilled. Ought to know better.'

Larsen lay where he was, propped on one elbow, thinking. Umiak needed warmth and medical attention urgently, but there was no way he could summon help. Even if he dared leave him it would be two days at least before he could summon any sort of aid, and by then it would be too late. He considered loading Umiak on the sledge and dragging him the last forty miles, but that, he figured, would be just another way of finishing him off.

'You'll have to leave me,' Umiak urged. 'Don't worry, I don't feel too bad as long as I lie still. No sense you waiting here until I die.'

'You're not going to die,' snapped Larsen impatiently. 'Lie quiet while I think.'

Umiak tried to laugh. 'You know that Presbyterian minister I told you about. He taught us to read and write and speak English. He was full of sayings. Always repeating them. One was "Hard work never killed anybody". Well, he was wrong. Hard work killed me.'

'You're not killed yet, for God's sake,' hissed Larsen. 'Now shut up, do. Save your breath and let me think.' He looked out over the valley. The wind had blown large areas almost clear of snow. Beyond the stream the hill showed black in the early light. There was bound to be plenty of dry wood there. Should he try to move Umiak? He was not sure he could make it, especially with the stream to cross. He would just have to leave him for a while and bring back as much firewood as he could carry. Then at least Umiak would be warm. He was tough, and maybe it was not pneumonia, just severe bronchitis. He didn't know.

If only he could raise help. If only a plane would pass over. Wryly he remembered his last attempt to attract attention, by making smoke. Suddenly he looked again at the hill across the valley. If only he could make enough smoke. A wild idea came to him. He knew it was Bureau of Land Management policy to fight all bush fires, which broke out with amazing frequency in the wilderness. Half the natives were employed all summer on fire-fighting duties. If he could start a bush fire, it should bring someone running.

If necessary, he thought, I'll set the whole goddamned mountain ablaze. He patted Umiak on the shoulder. 'I'm just going to get some firewood,' he announced. 'Shan't be long.'

There were two bags of petrol left, safely stowed in the holdall among the rocks. He checked that he had the lighter, and a length of cable with which to bind a bundle of firewood, and set off. The snow on the valley floor, where it remained, was firm and hard-packed by the wind, but it was slippery, and he had to walk with care. To his relief the stream scarcely covered the soles of his boots. The brush, when he reached it, was even denser and thicker than it had appeared from across the valley.

He worked methodically, building his starting fires with care, each one several yards apart. What little breeze there was blew up and aslant the hill, and he chose his sites accordingly, in a stand of cottonwood, at the base of a dead willow, among scrub birch and tall dry grass. There was kindling in plenty and he set aside as much as he thought he could carry back across the valley. He hoped there would not be much left after his work was done.

When he was satisfied he took the bag of petrol and punctured a small hole in the plastic. Fuel spurted out in a thin stream, and he went from fire to fire, soaking each one and laying a liquid fuse between each stack. Then, when the bag was empty, he threw it on the nearest one and flicked the lighter with his thumb.

The fires were slow to start. Larsen watched in an agony of apprehension as the flames spread, running through the undergrowth from wood-pile to wood-pile, flaring briefly, then dying, sulking, flickering briefly back to life. Then came a faint crackle and a flare. Flames began to leap and grow. Sparks flew skyward and dense black smoke began to rise. For a while the fire was contained in a line, and then rivers of flame began first to crawl and then to leap uphill. The growing heat created its own wind, the flames flared higher, and all at once the whole hillside seemed to explode with a roar and a blast of heat that sent Larsen staggering back. Then he could only stand in awe at the power and speed of the holocaust he had made. Smoke, dense black smoke, billowed up out of the flames, rising higher, and even higher. This time there was no flattening out as it reached the colder air. It towered skywards far above the mountain peaks. In the clear air it would be seen for miles.

Satisfied he had done all he could, Larsen turned his back on the blaze, picked up his bundle of sticks, and set off back across the valley. Halfway across he paused for a breather. The load was heavier than he had realized. Ahead of him was a wide expanse of unbroken snow, and now another idea came to him. Walking out into the centre of the snowfield he lay full length in the snow. Then he began to drag his body, snakelike, in a wide curve.

18

He had failed. Larsen sat dejectedly by the burning embers of the fire and looked out across the valley at the hill. From time to time brief outbreaks of flame blossomed on the mountainside, and a red glow showed where the undergrowth still smouldered, but the smoke pall had gone, faded beyond trace into the pale blue sky. He had cooked the last of their food and persuaded Umiak to drink some soup, but the hours had passed and still there had been no sign, no drone of a plane or the steady whop of a helicopter, to indicate that their signal had been seen.

They were both done for now. His leg was so bad he had barely been able to hobble back to the sledge. He didn't think it would carry him much further. He couldn't even bring himself to look at it. Behind him Umiak slept, but he was restless and disturbed, his breathing if anything faster and louder. From time to time he muttered in his sleep, but he would speak only in his native tongue, so that Larsen was unable to understand a word. He seemed delirious though, and had apparently forgotten the teachings of his old Presbyterian minister. Funny that, he thought. It explained the man's precise, almost pedantic way of speaking. He wondered if all Umiak's schoolmates spoke in the same way.

A raven flew over high in the sky. It circled the burned

hillside beyond the valley, and in a moment was joined by another. Soon several had gathered, no doubt waiting until the hillside cooled to gather the corpses of small animals and birds destroyed by the fire. Larsen shuddered, wondering what further carnage he had caused, wandering through the wilderness like some crazy pyromaniac. It occurred to him that what was food for the ravens was food for man, that he ought to make the effort to see what he could harvest for himself. Yet what was the point? The fatalism which seemed to have affected Umiak now gripped him too. He felt wrapped in a cosy sort of relief that their struggles were over. At least he had no further to walk.

Then he heard it, faint and far away, the sound of an aircraft high in the sky. As yet there was no way in which he could guess the direction of the sound, and slowly he stood up, staring skywards, gazing all round, his heart hammering wildly and his knees shaking beneath him. The sound grew fainter, then louder, until at last it filled his ears. Then the plane flew over the hill, a bright orange Piper twin. Larsen staggered out from the rocks and stood on a patch of snow, waving his arms as the plane roared over his head before turning and flying down the length of the valley. For a moment Larsen thought it was going to land, but evidently the pilot was reluctant to risk his undercarriage on the uneven rock-strewn floor. The Piper vanished over the mountains, and Larsen was alone in the silence once more. However, he knew now that he was saved, and he tried to tell Umiak the news, but the sick man did not seem to comprehend. Suddenly Larsen felt cold and alone and frightened. Since there was nothing else to do, he crawled back inside the bedding to wait.

He must have dozed a while for the roar of the snowmobiles was loud in his ears as he crawled out from their refuge. He watched them racing up the valley, thinking he'd never seen a sight more beautiful in his life. The driver of the leading vehicle brought his machine to a halt. He was a big guy, wearing sunglasses and a walrus moustache, his size accentuated by the bulky clothing he wore. He did not seem pleased to see Larsen. 'You guys have caused a heap of trouble,' he announced.

Larsen considered this for a while. 'I blame the weather,' he replied.

He came out of the anaesthetic to find Sylvie sitting at his bedside. 'What kept you?' he murmured.

Sylvie put her finger on his lips. 'Don't talk. Rest. Your leg is going to be all right. You'll need further surgery when the infection clears, but we'll fly you south for that.'

Larsen closed his eyes. 'How's Umiak?' he queried.

'Okay. He's very weak, but his temperature's down. I guess they found him just in time. He's pretty tough, though.'

He's tough all right, thought Larsen. Memories of the jolting, jarring ride back, sitting on a sledge towed behind a snowmobile, came drifting back. How Umiak had survived that ride he'd never know. The man had been right. It was not a comfortable way to travel. Dimly he remembered them being transferred to a plane. Where were they now, he wondered and, still wondering, fell asleep.

He woke refreshed and hungry and lay for a while dreaming of all the foods he would like to eat. In the end he had coffee and toast, and it was enough. Afterwards he felt restless and ill at ease. The air in the small sickbay was hot and stuffy after the cold Arctic air and the sheets seemed to hold him in soft suffocating bonds.

Sylvie arrived and fussed over him, arranging his pillows and running her fingers through his short sandy beard. Suddenly the thought of a shave seemed a luxury. 'Where's my gear?' he asked.

Sylvie's nose wrinkled in disgust. 'Your clothes are burned,' she replied. 'We emptied your pockets though. The stuff's here beside you.' She opened a drawer in the locker.

Larsen leaned over and found the arrow-head. 'Here,' he said, 'I promised you a souvenir.'

Sylvie held it up to the light. The stone was amber-coloured flint, translucent. 'It's beautiful,' she murmured. 'Where did you find it?'

Larsen told her. 'The mark of man's hand in the wilderness. Seemed to me that if he could survive, then so could I, but I wouldn't have made it without Umiak.'

'And but for you he would be dead by now. The pilot said that if you hadn't scraped that SOS in the snow he'd have kept going. The brush fire was almost out by the time he found it, and he didn't think it was worth reporting.'

Larsen remembered his long slow crawl through the snow.

'You mean nobody saw the smoke?'

'Oh sure, but they put it down to lightning strike. Often happens apparently, after a storm. They just checked it out as a matter of routine.'

'So he wasn't looking for us, then?'

'Why should he? Nobody dreamed you'd head east. When they eventually found the plane, they felt sure you'd head north, to the rig, but when you weren't there we looked south-west, thinking you'd made for the Howard Pass, and the Noatak. We were looking in all the wrong directions.'

'Umiak mentioned the Noatak,' said Larsen. 'Wait a minute. You said rig. What rig?'

'You didn't know?' breathed Sylvie. 'About twenty miles north of where you crashed, there's an airstrip and a drilling rig. You'd have been safe there. It's marked on the map.'

'The map blew away,' said Larsen wearily. 'Umiak

couldn't have known about it. Anyway, we didn't know where we were.' Suddenly he began to laugh. 'We sure took the pretty way home!'

Before he flew south he went to say goodbye to Umiak, now recovering well. Another visitor already sat by the bedside, a round, merry-faced man whose eyes were merely sparkling black slits squeezed in between high cheekbones and a brow. 'This is my friend I was coming to visit,' Umiak announced. 'The one the seal oil was for,' he smiled slyly.

Larsen, remembering how he had burned the seal oil, grinned ruefully. The stranger laughed and rubbed his ample paunch. 'No matter about the oil. I'm too fat already.'

'Nice of you to take it that way,' Larsen said. 'I wish I could feel the same about the souvenirs I was hoping to find in Anaktuvuk. It seems I shall be going away empty-handed.'

The stranger looked at him thoughtfully. 'Maybe I can help in that direction. I know of one or two people, good carvers in soapstone or deer antler, who might be interested in supplying you.' He took a piece of paper from his pocket and wrote on it with a stubby pencil before handing it to Larsen. 'Here's my address. Get in touch with me next time you're up this way.'

'Great,' Larsen said. 'I'll take you up on that. Thanks a lot.'

'Well, I'd do anything for a friend of Joe's, and Joe tells me you saved his life.'

'Joe?' Larsen looked sharply at Umiak, but the invalid had his eyes fixed firmly on the bedclothes, and would not meet Larsen's gaze. 'I'd been meaning to tell you,' he muttered, 'but with one thing and another...'

'Don't tell me,' scoffed his friend, 'you still believe in that old superstition about revealing your name. You'll be telling me you believe in shamans next.'

'I'm not sure he isn't a shaman himself,' said Larsen. 'Back there on the trail he turned himself into a caribou, right before my eyes, so he could carry a load of firewood across the snow.'

For a moment a flicker of unease crossed the little man's face. Umiak caught it and grinned wickedly at Larsen, who winked back.

'Hallucinations,' the other man retorted. 'Happens all the time in this country. Anyway, I must be off. I'll leave you two to swap fairy-tales. It's a wonder the pair of you didn't go off your heads if half of what Joe tells me is true. See you later Joe. Goodbye Mr Larsen, safe journey home, and thanks again for all you've done. I owe you.'

'I owe you too, Joe,' said Larsen softly.

'And I you,' said Umiak.

Larsen held out his hand, and Umiak took it in both of his, staring hard into his face. Suddenly embarrassed, Larsen could not think of anything else to say. 'You're looking pale,' he stammered at last.

'White man's food,' said Umiak, and they both laughed. 'By the way, I've been thinking. When you come back here to fix up a deal for those souvenirs, maybe we could make a proper hunting trip together.' He paused, grinning. 'We'll be fully equipped next time. I know of some fishing that would make your eyes pop. And maybe together we could plan a guided wilderness tour for some of your clients.'

'I'd like that,' replied Larsen. With a sudden sense of surprise, he realized that he meant it. He had lost his fear of the wilderness, and already he was feeling a faint itch to see more. He drew his hand away from Umiak's grasp. 'Before I forget,' he said, 'a little souvenir of our trip.' He put his hand in the pocket of his robe and pulled out the little penknife, dropping it into Umiak's lap. For a long time Umiak stared at it without speaking, then slowly his hand closed over it.

'Goodbye, Joe,' said Larsen.

'Goodbye . . . Steve,' said Umiak softly.

At the door Larsen turned back to wave. Umiak was already gazing thoughtfully at the knife, lovingly turning it over and over in his firm, strong hands.